My First Murder

NO. 1 IN THE MAVIS DAVIS SERIES

SUSAN P. BAKER

Books by Susan P. Baker

Novels:

My First Murder
No. 1 in the Mavis Davis murder mystery series

The Sweet Scent of Murder
Mavis Davis No. 2, Mavis's search for a missing teenager turns into a murder investigation in Houston's Ritzy River Oaks.

Death of a Prince
Mother & daughter criminal defense lawyers defend the alleged murderer of a millionaire plaintiff's attorney

Ledbetter Street
A mother fights the system for guardianship of her autistic son.

Suggestion of Death
A father who can't pay his child support investigates the mysterious deaths of other deadbeat dads.

UNAWARE
Attorney Dena Armstrong is about to break out from under the two controlling men in her life, unaware that a stranger has other plans for her.

Nonfiction:

Heart of Divorce
Divorce advice especially for those who are considering representing themselves.

Murdered Judges of the 20th Century
True stories of judges killed in America.

www.susanpbaker.com

ACKNOWLEDGMENTS

I would like to thank the (first) Galveston Novel and Short Story Writers Group for their support and friendship throughout the writing of this novel.

CONTENTS

Chapter 1

I COULD ALMOST FEEL MORE FRECKLES POPPING out on my face as I parked my Mustang and walked through the glaring morning sun to my office. It was hot for May. Too hot for me. I stooped down and grabbed the newspaper from where it lay on the steps and glanced at the front page before going inside. *THIRD WOMAN FOUND MURDERED* the headlines screamed. What a depressing way to start a day. Shoving the paper under my arm, I inserted the key in the lock and went into the cool of the air-conditioning before learning anything more about the deceased.

As usual, I was the first to arrive. So I entered the kitchen and, after piling my things on a chair, put the kettle on to boil. I then spread my morning paper across the kitchen table to read the murder article.

> *HOUSTON—Police are investigating an apparent murder after the strangled body of 36-year-old Doris Jones was discovered Tuesday morning.*
> *The victim, who failed to show up for work, was found in her apartment just after 6:00 a.m. by her employer, Carl Singleton.*

Jones lived alone above the cafe where she worked as a waitress for the past year. She was last seen alive on Monday night, Capt. Ronald Milton said.

Evidence found at the scene indicates that a struggle took place.

With Jones being the third woman strangled in less than a year, police now suspect a serial killer. Mary Lou Redmon's strangled body was found on Thanksgiving morning. The body of Susie Steinberger was found on Valentine's Day. All three of the women were in their midthirties and lived alone. See Murder, page 26A.

I wasn't comforted by the last line of the article. There was nothing I could do about my age, but perhaps it wouldn't hurt to begin looking for a roommate.

After brewing my cup of tea, I lit a cigarette and sat down at the table to scan the remainder of the news before I could be interrupted either by the arrival of my assistant, Margaret Applebaum, or, hopefully, by the jingling of the telephone. I should be so lucky. The phone hadn't rung in days. If the phone did ring, it was usually a wrong number.

All businesses have their ups and downs. Mine was down right now. Except for people dropping in to make Xerox copies, there didn't seem to be much sense in keeping the office open. I thought about discharging Candy, our little half-day high school helper. I hated to do it right before school got out. I knew she was relying on me for her summer job, but the income from photocopying wasn't enough to pay the utilities, and serving legal papers for lawyers was barely keeping us afloat—not to mention the lack of what I opened the business for, what was supposed to be our real work: investigations.

Being the eternal optimist that I am, though, I hadn't made the final decision yet. I just knew that any day now a paying client was going to walk through that front door, take one look at the professional decor of our offices, and hire us to do a difficult, and expensive, job. I was relying heavily on my optimism to get us by.

Admittedly, things were getting me down lately. Thank goodness I'd

2

had enough foresight to have a few sidelines, but even the typing service we offered was off. What was happening?

I scanned *Ann Landers* and the comics, didn't find anyone I knew listed in the obituaries, and was putting away the newspaper when Margaret finally showed up.

I heard the clanging of the cowbell that we had attached to the front door last year when a weirdo had silently slipped in on us. (But that's another story.) And then I heard Margaret call out to me, "Sorry I'm late, Mavis."

Yep, that's me. Mavis Davis. My mother had a sense of humor. I'm the owner/operator of *Mavis Davis Productions*. It says so right on the door in small print under the title, *Owned and operated by Mavis Davis*. I swear.

"It's all right, Margaret," I called back to her. "I was just finishing up with the paper."

"Anything exciting in the news?" she asked when she came into the kitchen to mix her instant coffee.

"Nothing more than a little murder," I answered as I turned to look at her.

"Murder, ugh."

"Wow! When did you do that?" I asked as I shielded my eyes from the glare of Margaret's freshly bleached-blond hair.

"Last night. Do you like it?" A hopeful expression on her face, Margaret twirled around so that I could get the full effect.

Not being an unkind person by nature, I hesitated to answer Margaret's query. The hair might have been stunning on someone else. It might even have been stunning on Margaret, but for the fact that Mother Nature had chosen to endow her with dark brown eyes and almost-black eyebrows that were too much of a contrast. I hate to say this, but it looked like a cheap wig. "It's a lovely shade of blond," I answered generously. "What made you decide to do it?"

"Well, with you being a redhead and all, and Candy normally having brown hair except when she sprays it green or blue, I thought I should be a blonde and add a little excitement to the office."

"Candy's hair is enough excitement for me, thank you very much."

"Aw, you hate it, don't you?" Margaret's lower lip jutted out as if she were about to cry.

"No, now I didn't say that. I expect it will grow on me, in time. It's just such a shock. You had a lovely head of black hair—much like I've often wished I'd been born with."

"I didn't know it would turn out quite this light," Margaret said a bit anxiously, the tears on the very verge of spilling out.

"I can imagine. Well, not to worry. I'm sure we'll all get used to it. Drink your coffee now and take your time with the paper. I'm going in to straighten up the office." I smiled at her encouragingly as I made my exit from the kitchen. I felt a little nauseated.

Not ten minutes later, after I'd emptied the waste baskets and removed the dust covers from the typewriters and our lonely little computer on which many payments were still owed, in came a large, blustering, red-faced man, whose brow was sweaty from the Texas heat.

He was dressed in navy polyester pants and a short-sleeved plaid sports shirt with the edge of a T-shirt peeking out over the top of the highest button he'd done up. He had stained running shoes on his feet, and he clutched a folded newspaper in a hand that was the size of a bear paw. I took one look at his attire, his crew cut, and his sleepy-looking blue eyes, and knew instantly that this was not the client of my dreams.

But, as I found out later, I was wrong.

"Good morning," I said pleasantly. I always greeted each person who came through that door as if they had an estate worth a million dollars. Let's face it, you never know.

The man grunted as he pushed the door closed behind him and came up to the counter behind which I stood with my best smile pasted on my face.

"What can I do for you this morning, sir?" I asked, anticipating that he wanted to photocopy an article out of the newspaper. What other logical explanation was there for carrying around the cumbersome Chronicle when it would have been ever so much more convenient to leave it in the car?

"I'm lookin' for Mavis Davis," his deep voice rumbled.

I flinched. I often still do when I hear my full name first thing in the morning. I keep thinking that someday I'll wake up and find that it was all a nightmare—that my mother didn't christen me so cruelly.

"I'm Miss Davis," I said radiantly, sticking out my hand for him to shake. "And you are?"

"Carl Singleton," he said, covering my not small hand with his paw and shaking it firmly. I like a firm handshake. It tells a lot about a person.

"Nice to meet you, Mr. Singleton," I said, withdrawing my hand. His name had a familiar ring to it. "What can I do for you?"

"I want to talk to you about investigating a murder," he said as he opened the paper and pointed to the front-page article I'd seen earlier. I wished that I'd read further.

It just goes to show you that you can never tell who may walk through the door. And possibly even that looks can be deceiving. This man was not exactly the client I'd envisioned. I have to tell you. He didn't look like he could afford to pay. Nevertheless, far be it from me to turn away anyone without hearing them out.

The expression on my face became appropriately serious as I contemplated Mr. Singleton's purpose in coming. Never before had I been involved with such an investigation. This could be my first murder.

Chapter 2

ANTICIPATION BEAT WILDLY IN MY CHEST. "Let me get my assistant in here to mind the store, so to speak, and then we'll go into my office where we can discuss this matter privately," I said. I hastened from behind the counter and darted into the kitchen to get Margaret who was frittering away precious time with her coffee and the newspaper.

"I've possibly got a live one, Margaret," I whispered fiercely as I passed through the swinging door into the kitchen. "Will you get out there and look busy while I talk to him in my office?"

Margaret must have heard the urgency in my voice and, knowing of our present financial plight, scooted out of her chair and followed after me, no questions asked.

"Now, Mr. Singleton," I said as I re-entered on the second swing of the door, "if you'll just follow me." I led the way through our little house-office to the only private room in the building, other than the bathroom and kitchen, that is.

As soon as I had him inside, I closed the door and indicated a chair opposite my desk. "Please have a seat," I said in my most professional manner as I circled around to my own. Plopping down, I crossed my legs, folded my hands, and said with deepest sincerity, "Now tell me. Exactly what is it that you'd like me to do?"

I peered across my orderly desk at the man, my eyes meeting his, and waited while he took a deep breath before he answered.

"Did you read the article in this morning's *Chronicle*?"

"Yes. About the third woman who was murdered? Yes, I did." It suddenly came to me why his name rang a bell. He was the employer of the recently departed woman.

"Her name was Doris. She worked for me for about a year—just like it said in the paper. And I want to know who killed her."

"You want me to try and find out?" I asked in a tone of voice that I hoped wasn't filled with incredulity.

"Yeah, 'cause I don't think the cops will find out who did it."

My adrenaline was pumping. "Mr. Singleton, if I recall the article correctly, the police are investigating the possibility of Miss Jones's death being the act of a serial killer. Should that prove to be true, the killer would be a person with no real motive, no vendetta, kind of like a random killer."

"They're wrong."

"What makes you say that?"

"I feel it in my gut."

It was a rather distasteful way of phrasing it, but as good as any.

"You'd have to know Doris. Know the way she was. It couldn't have been the same guy. She wouldn't have let just anyone in her apartment."

"Is that what they're saying? That she let someone in and whoever it was killed her?"

"Yeah. They think whoever did it has been posing as a repairman or something, but Doris wouldn't have let 'em in, at least not without checking with me first."

"There's no sign of a forced entry?"

"No none. Will you take the case?"

I hesitated while my brain worked ninety-to-nothing on a decision, my judgment clouded with dollar signs. Should I admit my inadequacies to the man? If I told him a little about myself, would he go away? How honest should I be in my hour of need? Real honest, I decided. I couldn't live with myself if I misled a person. I mean in a major way. I took a deep, regretful breath before answering.

"I don't know, Mr. Singleton. Actually, you see, I'm really not a real investigator—not that kind anyway. I could do the work, don't get me wrong, but what I mean is I'm not licensed for that. I mean, I am licensed for it. I have a Class A license, but it's for my experience in investigating child abuse and stuff." And I wanted to add, "and I'm really not into serial killings right now, Mr. Singleton, especially when the killer is doing away with women my age," but I didn't.

"I know. I checked you out."

"You did?" Sigh of relief.

"Yeah. I know all about you. And I like what I heard."

Flattery will get you everywhere. "Then you know my background, that I do home studies for adoptions, and social studies for child custody cases, and things like that."

"Yeah, and I know you used to be a probation officer, and a social worker, and that you studied criminology in college, and that sometimes you do investigations for lawyers around Houston."

My curiosity was aroused. I wondered how he knew so much about me. Would he tell me in time? I certainly wasn't going to exhibit poor taste by inquiring. "Mr. Singleton, what I do for lawyers—it isn't real investigation stuff. I talk to witnesses and sketch scenes for use in court, and I serve legal papers, but I don't try to find out who committed an offense. I do the background of a case when a lawyer is preparing for trial and needs information so that he or she can defend a client."

"It's the same thing," he said. "I know you can do it. I got faith in you."

I was wary of the job. Even if the man did have enough money to pay me a decent wage, he was asking me to look into a case while there was an active police investigation. I wasn't sure I wanted to do that. I was never one to court trouble. Well not too much trouble anyway.

I shook my head. "I appreciate your comments, Mr. Singleton, but why don't you let the police do their job first. Then, if they can't find out after a while who did it, I'll be glad to look into it for you." I pushed back my chair and stood up. I hated to end the interview, but I wasn't sure I was qualified to take on such a serious case. I also didn't want to tackle with HPD.

"C'mon, Miss Davis. You gotta help me. I know what the cops think, and they're wrong. I know she wasn't killed by no serial killer." His fingers gripped the edge of my desk as he leaned toward my face. "Please."

The desperation in his voice echoed throughout the room, taking me by surprise. Up until that point, I figured there was some angle to his request or that he thought I'd work cheap. Either way, I hadn't liked it. I'd felt uneasy. But now I sensed an urgency in him. Maybe there was something I didn't understand. I looked into his eyes again and saw an expression I took to be one of anguish. I wondered what Doris was to him anyway. So I asked him. "What was Doris Jones to you anyway?"

The big man lowered his eyes, looking down at his hands as if studying the size and shape of his fingernails. He didn't answer me.

"Well?" Suspicion is my middle name.

"Nothin'. She just worked for me, that's all."

"I suspect from your behavior that it was a little more than that," I told him as I took my seat again.

He raised his head and looked at me, his hands now twisting the newspaper into a tight roll. There was too much moisture in his eyes, and his mouth turned down at the sides. I could tell that it was hard for someone like him to talk about his feelings.

"She was something special, Doris was," he said at last. His voice was husky.

The room grew still and silent as I groped for words with which to ease his pain. His feelings for the woman were plain without his having to express them verbally.

"Will you tell me about her?" I asked, my voice almost a whisper in the quiet of the room.

He shifted around in his chair before answering, his eyes darting from object to object. Then he looked me straight in the eye and said, "Doris was a mystery to me."

Curious now, I asked, "What do you mean, 'a mystery'? A real mystery or was it just that she was a woman?"

"A real mystery," he said, and leaned forward to get closer to me. "She came out of nowhere last year and asked me for a job. She was quiet and sort of, well, elegant. I thought she'd add some class to the joint so I hired her even though I could tell she'd never waited tables before—she wasn't the type."

"Define 'quiet and elegant.'"

"Just what I said." He perked up. "She was always real quiet, never talked much to anyone, kept to herself. Not to say that she didn't do a good job. She was great. Best waitress *The Rex Cafe* ever had. She was always real polite to the customers, no matter what, and sometimes at night we get a real rough crowd in there. She could handle them; killed them with kindness, she did."

I must confess. He had me on a hook now and was reeling me in. Not to say that I was any more qualified than I was a few minutes earlier, but I was definitely interested. "It sounds like she was a very good worker," I commented, somewhat at a loss for an appropriate response.

"That's not the half of it." He had his elbows propped upon the front of my desk now, leaning toward me to tell me the story of Doris Jones. "The way she spoke, it was different. She talked like she had been somebody, like she had a real education. Kinda like you do. Sometimes she'd use big words that I didn't understand. I'd go look them up at night, only she didn't know it. But she didn't use 'em on purpose to make us feel stupid or nothin'; it was just like they'd slip out when she wasn't thinking about what she was saying. She'd try to cover up and change what she said so that we knew what she meant. She'd apologize and tell me that she was reading a lot of books and couldn't help it if she accidently learned some of the words, but I could tell that she was used to talking that way and having people understand what she said. You know what I mean?"

I nodded. "Where did she come from?"

"I dunno. Like I said, she was a mystery. I asked her more than once, but she only said something about being from north Texas and let it go at that. I knew her almost a whole year and can't tell you much more than I already have."

"What about her friends?"

He shook his head. "She didn't have any. Just us—the people she worked with at *The Rex*."

"I'll tell you, Mr. Singleton, what I think you need is a real detective. Why don't you go to Leo Barker or somebody? Some of those guys truly know the business and could probably help you find out about her." I hated to send him out to someone else, much as I needed the money, but he really did need somebody with more criminal experience, not little old me.

He shook his head again. "Leo Barker won't take the case. I already went to him yesterday."

I grimaced as my ego took a nosedive. "Well, there are others whose skills are equal to Leo's."

His head wagged from side-to-side. "No one'll touch it. They think I'm crazy. Actually, I think Leo would've except he's going on vacation for a couple of weeks and he said his wife would kill him if he didn't go this time. I don't want to wait no two weeks. The others, well, they had different excuses, but I could tell what they thought."

I had lost some of my sympathy for the man. I mean—it was quite a blow that I was at the end of a long list. I would have felt a good deal better had he not told me. But then, damn it all, I shouldn't have asked.

"Please, Miss Davis."

I was befuddled about the thing. In a quandary. Why shouldn't I refuse like the others? If they thought he wasn't all there upstairs, why should I think any differently?

Why? Because I needed the money.

Even so, I was still hesitant. "I don't know, Mr. Singleton. I'm sure the police are doing all they can to solve this thing."

"I'm telling you it's not part of the same case. It can't be. Doris knew better than to open the door to somebody off the street. Hell, the way she acted, she never even wanted to let us in there, much less some stranger."

"But what if it was some stranger? The serial killer. You'd be paying for

11

work that will be done by the police for free." I watched his face, hoping for a positive reaction.

"I don't care, Miss Davis. I have to have the answer. She was like a riddle. Even if a serial killer did do it, I still won't have the answer to Doris Jones. I want to know who she was. Could you just look into that part of it for me? Could you just help me find out who she was? I'll pay you. I have money saved 'cause I don't have a family or nobody to spend it on. I can pay you. At least look into it. You never know what you'll find. Please. I'm asking you. Maybe as a woman you'll be better anyway. Maybe you could unravel Doris's life."

So what else could I do? I mean, really? I needed the money. It would be better than sitting around the office waiting for a home study. I could at least look into it for the man; maybe spend a few days talking to people, snooping around. It might even be fun. I was still hesitant. I'm not sure why. My ego? No. Money is much more important. I guess I was a little scared because of the facts. But honestly, I have to admit it was interesting. The mystery woman. And what if it turned out to be more than interesting? I might be able to make a name for myself. This might be the beginning of something. It could be my big break. I might become a real investigator: a criminal investigator.

So what was I waiting for?

I was trying to decide how much to charge for snooping around for a few days.

"I'd have to charge you thirty-five an hour plus expenses," I said, cringing internally as I anticipated that he'd change his mind.

As I looked on, he stood up, dug his hand into his pocket, and pulled out a wad of bills. He peeled a bunch off and laid them on the desk in front of me. "Here's seven hundred. It's Wednesday, and that should cover the rest of the week. Let me know if you need more."

I was simply astonished. He must have really loved her. Maybe I should have quoted a higher hourly rate. "I'm not promising you anything, you understand, Mr. Singleton. I'll look into it for you. I'll ask around a little and see what I can come up with that will convince you that her death was part of a serial killing. I'll check on her background. I can't guarantee anything more than that."

A huge grin spread across his face. "It's a start, Miss Davis," he said. Then, much to my surprise—and before I knew what was happening—he came around my desk and gave me a big wet smack on the cheek, squeezed my shoulders, and was gone.

Chapter 3

IT TOOK ME A FEW MINUTES to fully recover from the shock of being hired on a real murder case, but when I snapped out of it, I was raring to go. I gave Margaret Applebaum some instructions for tasks for her and Candy to carry out during the remainder of the day, clipped the article out of the *Chronicle*, and headed for the newspaper office downtown. I wanted to read the back issues for details on the other murders.

What drudgery. After hours of reading, my research into the deaths of Mary Lou Redmon and Susie Steinberger didn't turn up much that I considered helpful.

Mary Lou Redmon had lived alone in a singles complex in northeast Houston. She was thirty-five years old, divorced, and had no children. She made her living as a bookkeeper at a small downtown office.

Susie Steinberger was thirty-four years old and had lived in a duplex off Westheimer. She was a cocktail waitress at a bar in Pasadena, which was quite a bit south of where she lived. She had been thrice divorced. One of her ex-husbands had custody of the only child she had ever borne, a boy aged fourteen. They lived in Oregon.

Both women had been raped and strangled in their homes.

Both bodies were discovered on holidays, Mary Lou's on Thanksgiving, Susie's on Valentine's Day.

Mary Lou was short, slightly overweight, and had brown hair.

Susie was tall, underweight, and had bleached-blond hair.

I didn't know what connection the police had found between the two to make them think the deaths were serial killings unless there was something that was not reported in the newspaper. The first thought that came to mind was that the semen specimens matched. Somehow I'd have to finagle that information. I jotted down one last note in my spiral notebook before returning to the world of the living.

I stepped outside the newspaper offices, my head in a fog as I thought about the dead women, and was greeted by a blast of hot, humid, Houston air. My eyes burned from the glare of the sidewalk. My stomach rumbled with hunger, and I realized that I'd worked through the noon hour. I stopped and lit a cigarette while I tried to make another decision. I was anxious to get over to Doris Jones's apartment to have a look around, but at the same time, my stomach was arguing with my brain. We compromised. I'd grab a sandwich and eat it in the car.

I never was much good at doing two things at the same time. As I walked toward the car, I was fumbling for my sunglasses and keys when I literally ran headlong into my old drinking buddy, Fred Elliot, whose huge mass was like a barricade across my path.

Fred was a reporter for the *Chronicle*. He used to be assigned to the courthouse beat when I was an adult probation officer. He was always hanging around trying to get information on criminal cases to put in the paper or else waiting to hear a politician put his foot in his mouth. I hadn't seen him since I'd left the county payroll, but I'd heard a rumor that the previous year he'd gotten too personally involved in some political goings-on and was switched to another beat.

"What are you doing in my neck of the woods, Mavis?" he asked me after our initial greeting and a kiss on the cheek. My cheek, not his. His was dripping perspiration.

I looked up at Fred's friendly face and formed an idea. Maybe—just maybe—Fred would know a little more about the murders than what was printed in the newspaper. He was like that, just a well of information. I was going to drop my dipper in and see what I pulled out. "Just doing a little research job for a client," I answered and turned on the charm. I also shuffled the notebook in my arms and placed the article about Doris Jones on top, where he could see it.

"You mean your business is actually making it? I thought surely you'd be back at the county before too long. I've missed seeing you."

I grinned, hoping to dazzle him with my brilliant smile. "You know me, Fred. Once I make up my mind to do something, I stick it out. Besides, they wouldn't take me back now on a bet." Fred laughed and encircled my shoulders with an arm. "Told them what you thought again, did you?"

I shrugged my shoulders, hoping he'd take the hint. Speaking for myself, I never wanted more than a father-daughter relationship. "Yeah. The day they told me I didn't have time to counsel with the probationers—that the paperwork was more important than the people—was the day I made up my mind to get out. Probation has become just a bunch of bureaucratic bullcrap. But that's old news, Fred. Listen, I'm fixin' to find something to eat. Want to come along so we can do some catching up?"

"Sure. Which way are you headed?"

"I don't know. I was going to get a sandwich, but is there any place around here that serves a decent plate lunch?"

"Nope. There's a cozy little restaurant around the corner though. Come on girl; we can talk better on a full stomach."

I cocked my head at Fred to let him know that my feelings about a relationship with him hadn't changed. He smiled an acknowledgment, then led me to a little vine-covered restaurant, which from its appearance and that of the late lunch crowd that was still on the premises, was apparently a haven for newspaper folks.

We squeezed behind a corner table just inside the door and, except for interruptions from all the backslappers, had a good lunch. I managed to glean from Fred that he was on the police beat now. I couldn't fathom why he hadn't commented on the Jones article. He had to have seen it. I left it in plain view off to the side of the table, knowing how nosey reporters are.

Finally, I decided, the heck with it, and asked him point-blank, "Fred, what do you know about the murder of Doris Jones?"

Fred's pretty cool, and I could tell he didn't want to indicate that he knew much. He kept his reaction down to one of mild surprise, barely even raising his bushy gray eyebrows. "Isn't that the dame they found murdered yesterday morning?"

"C'mon, you know it is. You're probably the one who wrote the article with no byline in this morning's Chronicle." I grinned at him. I was never one to play a game too awfully long. "Besides, I've been flaunting the clipping since I ran into you, and I know you better than that. It's just too obvious that you've been ignoring it."

Fred's large face broke out into a toothy smile. "You've got me, Mavis. I guess I should have asked why you're carrying it around, huh?"

To which I nodded my head self-assuredly.

"So why are you carrying that clipping around?"

"I asked first, Fred. What do you know about it?"

Fred shook his shaggy head. "Looks like we're in a Mexican standoff. I'll tell you if you'll tell me, but we're both going to have to keep it under our hats. It's Captain Ron's case."

"Who the heck's Captain Ron?"

"Girl, you have been gone a long time! Captain Ronald Milton of HPD." He pointed to the name in the article. "His team of detectives is investigating it, and he doesn't like anyone snooping around. It's harder than hell finding out any information from his people, 'cause they know if they get caught, there'll be hell to pay. He's the most secretive son-of-a-bitch in the police department."

I guess disappointment showed in my face. I sure felt it. It was going to be harder than I thought finding out anything for Mr. Singleton. I must have let out an audible sigh, because Fred said, "That bad, huh?"

I looked up at him across the table. "Yeah. I promised this guy I'd look into it for him."

Fred patted my hand. "Well, don't give up. I'll tell you all I can."

"Thanks, Fred. I'm not. I guess in my dreams I thought it would be easy being a criminal investigator. I'm still going to snoop, and I promise you I'll give you anything I find if you'll help me."

"So who's your client? What does he want to know?"

"Uh, I don't think I can tell you who he is. Ethics—right?"

He nodded and grinned, his smile wrinkles showing up again in his meaty face. I guess he thought I was dumber than I am.

"Suffice it to say that I'm being paid to find out for sure if Doris Jones was the third in a series of killings, and to look into her background, find out all I can about her."

"I can tell you this, Mavis. HPD is considering bringing in a psychologist to do a profile on the killer. They really do suspect it's a serial."

"But why? What's the connection between them? There are murders almost every day in Houston. What ties these three together?"

"The dope isn't all in on Jones, but I can give you what I have on the first two. I promised not to print it yet, but there was a semen match for Redmon and Steinberger."

"That's what I thought."

"Also, all three of them were strangled with stockings."

"Really? That's interesting. Their own stockings? Like panty hose?" What a repulsive thought. I hoped the crotch was clean.

"I don't know," Fred answered, shaking his head again. "I can't seem to get more than that out of my source. I keep trying. Now you tell me. Why is your client interested?"

"You promise to keep it under your hat?" I put my most serious expression to work on my face.

"Sure. We made a deal, didn't we?"

"Yeah, okay" I don't know why I hesitated. I had to trust Fred if he was trusting me. "Fred, it seems there's a mystery surrounding Doris Jones. My client says that she came out of nowhere, and he wants me to find out about her life before she came to Houston. He's adamant that her murder was not part of the others."

"What is he basing that on?"

"Gut feeling."

"That's it? That's all you have?"

"Yes. I just started this morning. But if there's any reason to suspect that she wasn't killed by the same guy well, I need to know it before I get any deeper into this."

"Hey, Mavis, that's tough, because the cops aren't going to tell you if they do know. Even if it was a separate murder, it still falls under the jurisdiction of Captain Ron."

"Well, I have to try. I've been paid, and as far as I'm concerned, the money is spent."

We gathered up our things and went back out into the heat with a promise to keep each other posted on anything else that came up. Plus, Fred extracted a promise from me that I wouldn't do anything that would put me in danger. Although he's wanted to be more, Fred's like a father to me.

As I walked the six blocks back to where I had parked my classic car, I pondered my next move. Knowing that I couldn't go down to the police station and barge in with questions, I decided to go out to *The Rex Cafe* to have a look around Doris' apartment. Maybe I could make a start on her background search by seeing how she lived.

Chapter 4

EXPECTED TO SEE A RUN-DOWN TWO-STORY building that housed a greasy-spoon cafe, and I wasn't disappointed. The exterior of *The Rex* was badly in need of a paint job. The white paint was cracked and peeling off the wood. A large plastic red and white coke sign with the name of the cafe printed on it in black letters hung down on a post above the entrance. Off to the right was a set of stairs that I suspected led up to Doris' living quarters.

I had to go inside the cafe to get the key. I opened the wood-framed screen door and then a wooden door with a glass window in which a plastic open sign hung from a nail. To my surprise, the interior was a lot more modern than I expected. And cleaner, too.

To my right and left were rows of booths. Pink plastic rosebuds in narrow, imitation-milk glass vases were centered on bright tablecloths. Four-top and eight-top tables were lined up neatly on the main part of the floor with Samsonite chairs surrounding them. Overhead was modernized recessed lighting.

At the back was the kitchen where I could see Carl through a serving window. He was moving around, intently concentrating on something that was, undoubtedly, someone's meal, which explained the stains on his running shoes. He hadn't told me he was the cook.

I made my way to the kitchen entrance and stood there for a minute watching him. He wore a large white apron that covered him from neck to knees and was tied at the waist. He was garnishing a plate with an orange slice and a sprig of parsley. When he finished, he put the plate up in the window and hit a little bell; then I caught his attention.

"Nice place you've got here," I said, gesturing.

The corners of his mouth turned up slightly, in a melancholy little smile as he glanced through the window. "Yeah, Doris helped me redecorate, kind of brighten up the place, you know? She had a lot of good ideas."

"I was wondering if I could get a look at her apartment," I said bluntly. I was never one to mince words.

"Sure," he replied, reaching under his apron. I heard the jangle of some keys and then he separated one out and gave it to me. "I don't know what you'll find that the police ain't already seen, but go ahead."

Shrugging, I said, "I don't know either, Mr. Singleton, but it's worth a look. At least maybe I can get an impression of her from it."

"Carl. Call me Carl."

I smiled at him. "Only if you call me Mavis."

"It's a deal. You found out anything yet, Mavis?"

"Not much. I did a little reading about the other two murders and have been asking around. I'll let you know if I learn anything significant. I have an angle I'm working on."

"I'm not trying to rush you. I know it's only been a few hours."

A waitress in a pink uniform and a small, ruffled, white apron came up to the window and retrieved the plate, replacing it with a ticket. She stared at me and nodded her head, but didn't speak. I nodded back, knowing that eventually I would have to talk to her and everyone else associated with the cafe. I was saving that for after I saw the apartment.

"Guess I'll go on up and have a look. Okay if I come back and talk to some of your employees later?"

"Sure. Holler if you need anything, Mavis. Anything at all," Carl said, and then reached for the ticket, his attention turned to preparing the next meal.

As I went out, I saw three waitresses sitting together at a table near the cash register. They were watching me intently. I smiled broadly at them, hoping to set the tenor of our future conversation. I was hoping they wouldn't be paranoid about talking with me. They each smiled in return.

I climbed the stairs to the apartment door and inserted the key that Carl had given me. The door opened easily into a large living area. I pushed it closed behind me, and stood there, trying to get a solid first impression of what I saw. It was not a very large place, but looked somewhat comfortable. There was a sofa, a TV, and books.

It wasn't two minutes later that the door I had just closed crashed open behind me. I must have jumped a mile high.

"What do you think you're doing in here?" A gruff voice barked from behind me.

I thought I recognized it. I prayed that I didn't.

Chapter 5

TURNING AROUND, I CAME FACE-TO-FACE WITH one of the sorriest excuses for a police officer that I have ever known: Lon Tyler. He was glaring up at me, his fierce brown eyes sunken into a head that always appeared to me to be too large for his squatty body. His dark hair was pasted to his head with sweat that I could smell from two feet away. The underarms of his shirt were stained in huge circles. He stood there, hands on his hips, feet spread apart, an angry snarl on his lips, and looked as if he was going to order me to *assume the position* so he could frisk me.

Creeps. I had a feeling of deja vu. For a minute I felt as if I were back on my college campus some fifteen—uh, or twenty—years earlier at a busted sit-in.

I had to think fast to come up with a cover story. I didn't like Lon. Never had since a run-in with him a few years earlier when I was a probation officer. I let him know that I thought he was too violent with defendants.

Lon didn't like me either. Called me The Social Worker. He always thought he was Mister Perfect. I always thought he had a Napoleon complex and couldn't stand the way I towered over him. It gave me great pleasure now to have the opportunity to look down at him once again. I was especially pleased that I'd chosen two-inch heels to wear with my dress.

"Lon," I called his name in my most melodious voice and held out my hand for him to shake. "How are you? Long time no see."

He didn't fall for it. He ignored my outstretched arm and repeated himself. "I said, what are you doing here?" he snarled.

"Here?" I asked, all wide-eyed innocence. "Oh—you mean in this apartment? Well, really, what business is it of yours?" My brain was doing overtime trying to come up with some logical reason for my presence.

"Police business, that's what," he spouted.

"Police business? Oh because of what happened to the last tenant. I see. Yes. I read about that in this morning's paper. Poor thing. How's the investigation going, Lon? They got you on it?"

"That's none of your business. Now you want to tell me what the hell you think you're doing?"

"Sure, Lon. I was thinking of leasing the apartment. I talked to Mr. Singleton downstairs and he said it would be all right if I had a look around. It's a nice place, isn't it?" I was flashing the friendliest smile I could muster and hoping that my shiny blue eyes would take him in at least a tad. I hadn't gotten more than a few steps inside when I was interrupted. Really—I hadn't seen a thing. It was a shame Lon was such a tough nut.

"Look, Mavis Davis," he said, uttering my name in such a nasty way that I wasn't pleased, "you're up to something. I can just feel it. I've had my eye on you for a long time. I know you couldn't make it at child welfare or the probation department and went out on your own. I don't know what you think you're doing, but you'd better not be messing around in my case. You're not interested in renting this apartment any more than I am, and I want you to clear out right now." With that, he held the door open and pointed toward the stairs.

Talk about adding insult to injury. It was all I could do to maintain my facade. "No, Lon—really. I've been looking for a new place. I haven't been happy with Montrose lately, know what I mean?" It didn't work, didn't fool him for one iota. But what the heck, I had to give it my best shot.

"Out!" he said in a voice so loud it made my ears ring. What can I say? I departed.

Back into the cafe I went to tell Carl what had transpired so that he could cover for me. He was still making meals in the kitchen so I hastened to him in case old Lon decided to give Carl the third degree.

"Hey." I peeked my head through the door and caught Carl's eye. "Did you tell anyone that you hired me?"

"Only the girls here. Why?" Carl asked as he came over to where I stood. I could smell the aroma of fried food on his clothes, but it was better than what I smelled on Lon.

I grimaced. "I didn't any more get inside the door than a cop came in and ordered me out. You didn't tell me they were still watching the place, that they weren't through with it. Do you think the girls told the cops about me?"

"No. I swear they wouldn't do that. We didn't know, Mavis. They didn't say anything about it. You didn't get a chance to look around?"

"No. Listen, they must have him parked across the street watching the place, so there's no way I can get back in without their knowing about it. I told him that I was thinking of leasing the apartment from you. Can you handle that story?"

"Sure, and I'll tell the girls. Say, I've got a key to the back door; you want to use it?"

"I don't know, Carl. I'd better not right now. I have a feeling that if I don't leave here pretty quickly, Detective Tyler, and I use that term loosely, is going to come find out the reason why. Are you sure you don't just want to continue with the cops investigating it? It appears they're taking it pretty seriously." I was feeling awfully disappointed about the thing, I must say. I had wanted to come up with something quickly. I wanted to impress Carl with my ability.

"Hey, we've got a deal, Mavis. You can't give up on me that easily. I hired you for the rest of the week and I expect you to earn that money," he said in a kind voice. It was as if he could read my face.

I sighed. Yes, sighed. I wasn't sure where to go from there. The initial excitement had worn off. No more adrenaline.

"Okay, Carl. You're right. You hired me to do a job this week, and I'm gonna do it. I'll be back at my office this afternoon if you need me. Otherwise, I'll call you tomorrow."

I went out, sure that Lon Tyler would be watching. I scanned the street and spotted him in a parked car at the corner. I grinned and waved to him. The son of a gun.

Back at the office, I gathered my little group around me for a brainstorming session. I thought three heads were better than one, and maybe together we could come up with some decent ideas. We were a colorful group, me with my carrot-colored hair, Margaret with her lemon-yellow, and Candy, who had chosen a lovely shade of blue that day.

We congregated behind the counter, sitting at the circle of desks, elbows on typewriters, and stared at each other. I explained the job to them, for in my haste to get started that morning, I hadn't stopped to tell Margaret much about it, and of course Candy hadn't yet arrived from school then.

"Gee, like this is really bad, Mavis!" Candy exclaimed after I told them about the mystery surrounding Doris Jones. "It's like *Madame X.* Did you ever see that movie?" Needless to say, Candy is an old movie buff.

"I fail to see the similarity, Candy. In *Madame X*, the heroine, so to speak, killed someone. In this case, this lady was killed," I said, the pain that was growing in my head and elsewhere making me frown at her.

"Yeah, but Mavis, both of them were hiding something, right? The lady in *Madame X* was trying to protect her family from what she'd turned into. You know? What had Doris Jones turned into? Was there something wrong with her? Maybe she was a drunk or killed somebody. What had she run away from?" Candy's enthusiasm was overwhelming. She was like an animated character out of the cartoons when she spoke, brown eyes flashing, head bobbing, earring dangling. Today she only wore one, a huge loop.

Margaret chimed in. "Did she look like Lana Turner?"

"Give me a break," I said, turning to Margaret. But Candy was right, we didn't have enough information. Heck, we didn't have any. I could see right off that I was going to have to go back and have a long talk with Carl and the waitresses.

I rolled a sheet of typing paper into the typewriter. "Let's do a profile of Doris Jones. Let's make a list of all the questions we have about her and fill in the answers as we get them, okay?" I typed her name at the top of the paper.

"Budge over, Mavis," Margaret said as she shifted from her chair toward mine. "You talk; I'll type. I want to feel useful."

"Okay." I stood up. "What do we need to know about Doris Jones, and what do we already know?" I began pacing the floor. "Candy, you really sort of hit the nail on the head. I don't know if she drank. Maybe she was using drugs. And Margaret," I said in an apologetic tone. "I really don't know if she looked like Lana Turner or not. I didn't get a photograph of her or even a description from Carl. My brain must have taken a hike. Let's get organized."

Margaret's fingers were flying across the keys as I spoke. I gave her a minute to catch up. Candy perched on the edge of the desk, leaning forward as if about to sprint.

Margaret stopped, pulled the paper from the typewriter, got up, and went over to the computer, turning it on. She slipped in a couple of disks. "I'm going to do the list on the computer so I can rearrange our questions by category when we get through. I wish, now, that I had a program that would somehow do profiles on people," Margaret said.

In spite of what she looked like, Margaret was a computer whiz.

"Sometime when it's really slow, Mavis, I'm going to design a program like that. I've been thinking about doing it for our child-custody studies. You know, feed the computer the characteristics about the ideal home situation for a child and then the characteristics about both parties wanting custody?" She was punching keys as she spoke and then looked up.

I felt a little stab in my head as Margaret rambled on. "That's a great idea, Margaret. Are you ready now?"

"Yes. I've listed things we need. Like a picture. Now what do we really know about her?"

"She was a white female aged thirty-six," Candy piped up.

"She was a waitress for almost a year. She came from northern Texas, Carl said. She was secretive, quiet, elegant, a real lady. She was well-read or else had a good education," I said.

By this time, Candy and I were standing behind Margaret watching the screen as she quickly punched in the information we were giving her.

"Did she own a car? Have any bank accounts or charge accounts?" Candy asked.

"Those are some of the things I need either to ask or get into her apartment to find out." I had told them about my run-in with Lon Tyler.

"She was strangled," Candy put in.

I grimaced at the thought. "With a stocking. Sometime between the hours of well, I'm not sure what time Monday night, write that down, Margaret, but she was found around six Tuesday morning."

"Was she raped, Mavis?" Candy asked, her eyes meeting mine over the top of Margaret's head.

In spite of Candy's weird hair and wild clothes, she was still a kid. I couldn't help but feel that a seventeen-year-old girl shouldn't know about such things. I mean, the way society is today, kids know about violence, but it's a shame. I shrugged at Candy and then reached over and patted her on the arm. "I don't know." I needed an aspirin. "Write that question down, Margaret."

"Maybe Ben could find out," Margaret said, turning and looking up at me from her perch.

"Omigosh, Ben!" In the excitement of it all, I had forgotten about him. My head pounded. Benjamin Sorensen, my amour. My big hunk of a man. Sergeant Benjamin Sorensen, HPD Narcotics Division. Who thought we should get married. Who thought I should stay home and have babies. Who wouldn't like the idea that I was looking into a murder. I glanced at Margaret, then at Candy. "No. I don't think so. Listen, you guys, you know how Ben is. I think we'd better keep this to ourselves."

But it was too late.

Chapter 6

T WASN'T AN HOUR LATER THAT Ben called up and asked me to dinner. And in order to act normal, I went, headache and all.

I could tell when Ben picked me up that something was wrong. He didn't say what it was right away, but as we drove to the restaurant, he was silent. I could see him clenching his jaw. When he did that, I knew I was in for it.

I kept trying to catch his eye. I made little jokes, but he didn't laugh. Normally he has some semblance of a sense of humor. I watched his large face for some sign, some clue to what was bothering him. I reached across the table for his hand, but he pulled it away.

Finally, I came right out and asked him. What the heck, I didn't have anything to lose at that point. Or so I thought.

"What in the hell do you think you were doing over at that dead woman's apartment?" he demanded. His chocolate-brown eyes were narrow slits, boring intensely into mine like tiny laser beams. His balled up fists were pressed on the edge of the table. His lips had formed into thin little lines as he gritted his teeth at me.

Hoo-boy! I felt like I'd grabbed a live wire. I'm afraid I reared back in my chair as if slapped. Never had I seen him quite so angry. I was, at first, speechless. For me, that's saying a lot.

Our dinner dishes having been cleared away, there was no barrier between us, and we stared into each other's faces for what had to have been a good two minutes. Neither of us spoke. I found that I was holding my breath while my mind was once again racing to find a rational explanation for my presence in the apartment.

"How did you know?" I asked finally, thinking at the same time that the answer was obvious.

"My captain told me," he said. "Right before he chewed my ass out. He got a call from the homicide captain."

Jeez. I could just see the chain of events. Lon Tyler told his captain, who told Ben's captain, who really told Ben, and now Ben was telling me. My inclination was to slip under the table, away from the scrutiny of Ben's eyes.

"So you got some smart answer to give me about why you were there?" he asked, still with an unpleasant tone of voice. "I already heard about the one you gave Tyler."

"Gee, honey, I'm just trying to make a living," I answered in my most pitiful voice. "You know how bad business has been lately." I cast my eyes down at the tablecloth and slumped my shoulders just a bit as I waited for his response.

"You ought to have a real job," he muttered in his deep voice, but I could tell that the anger was leaving him. "Who's paying you and to do what?"

Now was my chance. If I worked it just right, I might be able to find out what Ben knew. I would have to be careful not to step on the police department's toes, though. I spoke to him in my softest little-girl voice. "I've been hired to look into Doris Jones's background, to find out where she came from before here. I've been hired by someone who loved her very much and who just wants some answers to some questions. I can't tell you who. My client wants me to keep it a secret. They don't mean any harm. They just want to know about her."

"I'm not buying that, Mavis," Ben said in a cynical voice. "It's true, Ben," I said as I looked into his eyes as earnestly as possible. They had opened up a bit, indicating to me that the storm was probably over. "They haven't hired me so much to find out who killed her, but to find out more about her."

"Why? Is there some great mystery about Doris Jones, the waitress?" He raised one eyebrow at me, skeptical.

"Yes. Ben, I'm telling you the truth. There is a mystery. She showed up out of nowhere last year, and this person simply wants to satisfy a curiosity as to who she really was. She wasn't your typical waitress. They say that she was sort of hiding out. She was very secretive about herself."

"This is one of the weirdest stories that you've ever come up with, Mavis."

I shook my head at him. What could I do to convince him that I wasn't lying? Why did it seem that he didn't trust me? "It's true, Ben. You've got to believe me." By this time, I was almost pleading with him.

"If it's true, why'd they go to you instead of some of the real detective agencies in town?"

"He did," I answered. "They thought it was a weird story, too, and wouldn't help. I was their last hope. Don't you see? I couldn't turn 'em down. No one else would help."

"I don't know, Mavis," he said, giving me a sideways look. "It smells pretty fishy to me."

"Ben! This person was devastated at the idea that this woman was raped and murdered! He—they want to do something about it. If she was done away with by a serial killer, they'll accept that, but they need to know for sure. Even so, they want to know what brought her to where she was when she died. Don't you see? I have to continue on. I have to find the answers." I was so angry that I wanted to shake him. What would it take to convince him?

I scrutinized his face. He appeared to be getting angry again, but I didn't care. I was going to do my job and no one was going to stop me.

Ben's face turned red as he suddenly exploded at me, pointing his finger almost up my nose. "Mavis, you just can't go around messing in official police business! We're already investigating it. We've got Tyler and some other men on it. We've had an autopsy and found out that she wasn't raped. She was just strangled." He stabbed his finger at me. "We're doing our job.

We'll find out who murdered her without your help! I'm telling you to butt out of it, and I mean it!"

I started to yell back at him, mindless of the fact that we were still sitting in the middle of a reputable restaurant, when suddenly his words sank in. She wasn't raped. He said she wasn't raped. I was stunned. Could it be that Carl was right? That she wasn't murdered by the serial killer? I glanced back at Ben's face. I could almost see the smoke billowing out of his nostrils. He didn't realize what he'd let slip. I was excited now, my anger gone, but I couldn't let Ben know how I was feeling. I had to keep up a facade. I wanted to smile at him, give him my thanks for convincing me that Carl wasn't a nut, but I gritted my teeth and wrung my hands and pretended I was still fighting. "I don't think you have the right to ask me not to look into Doris Jones's background," I said.

Ben reached out again and I reared back from his finger. "I'm not asking you. I'm telling you, Mavis. Keep out of it."

I slid out of my chair and stood up. The only thing to do at this point was go home. I had to get away from Ben before he realized that the fight had gone out of me. As coldly as possible I said, "I'll consider it," and I turned and started walking toward the door.

Ben quickly paid the check and hurried after me. On the way home, we didn't speak. I didn't ask him in. I couldn't. Let's face it, I'm better at avoidance than confrontation. As he drove away, I wondered whether there would be a continuation of our relationship. But I couldn't be bothered with that now. I'd think about that tomorrow, like Miss Scarlet. Right now, I had more serious things to ponder. Like, if it wasn't the serial killer, who murdered Doris Jones?

Chapter 7

THE NEXT DAY I PHONED CARL to tell him I was coming over with some good news. Not only did I wish to speak to Carl, but my goal for the day was to get into Doris' apartment if it killed me. Well, not quite if it killed me, but I intended to take drastic measures.

Knowing that Lon Tyler would be lying in wait for me, I ransacked my closet for a disguise. Thank goodness I never let my mother break me of being a pack rat.

I found some old one-inch brush curlers and rolled my hair up in them. Then I covered it with silver hair spray I'd kept from the time I went to a costume party as a bag lady. Over that mess, I tied a madras babushka, a relic from when I was a surfer girl on the Galveston waves. I pulled on an old pair of jeans, tennis shoes, and an oversized shirt that could have been my daddy's, and touched off the disguise with a pair of huge reflecting sunglasses. I only hoped that Carl would appreciate my ingenuity and not question his decision to hire me.

The air was already insufferably hot that morning, and there was no gulf breeze blowing in from the South. The humidity was probably at an all-time high of 150 percent. I was miserable as I drove down the Gulf Freeway. I'd been having problems with the air-conditioning in my car. Some days it chose to work. Some days it didn't. Today was one of those days it chose to torture me. By the time I reached my destination, I was drenched with perspiration and praying for rain to cool things off. Luckily my hair was in curlers, or the humidity would have made it look like bedsprings.

I parked two blocks north of *The Rex* so that Lon wouldn't spot my car, an unforgettable yellow with a black convertible top. When I reached the block on which the cafe sat, I saw Lon, still perched at the corner like a public fixture waiting for a dog to come along and christen it.

I had beaten the lunch crowd so that I could have some time alone with Carl. As I made my way to the rear of the cafe, my appearance drew a lot of attention. I pulled my glasses down and waved at the waitresses as they stared at me. They cracked up.

At the entrance to the kitchen, I stopped. I have an aversion to kitchens; I never want to spend too much time in or near one. Carl was sitting on a stool reading the newspaper. "Hi," I said, causing him to glance at me. A curious expression formed on his face. It tickled me.

"Can I help you?" Carl asked.

I laughed and pulled off my sunglasses.

"Well, I'll be," Carl said and smiled broadly.

"Didn't recognize me, did you?"

"Nope. What're you doing in that getup?"

"Fooling the cops, what else? Can we talk?"

Carl shook his head in apparent disbelief as we went to sit at a corner table out of earshot of the others.

"Carl." I spoke his name soberly after we were seated and, getting his attention, placed my hand on his large forearm. "She wasn't raped."

Perhaps I should have eased into that particular piece of news, but I didn't. I hadn't expected the reaction it drew. Carl's head dropped down, his chin on his chest, and he uttered such a loud sob that it startled me. He pulled his arm away and covered his face with his hands for a minute while he recovered himself. Silently, I waited for him to speak.

He let out a long, shuddering sigh and then took a paper napkin from the tin, wiped his face and eyes, and blew his nose. "I'm so glad," he said hoarsely.

I could tell that he had loved her very much.

Then he said, "You believe me now, don't you, Mavis?"

"I believed you yesterday."

"No—no, you didn't. You were just humoring me and you needed the money, but you believe me now, don't you?"

What could I say?

"What's next?" he said.

"I really need to get into her apartment, Carl, but I've been warned away. Can you get me in the back door?"

"Sure. Want to go now?"

"In a few minutes. I don't want that police officer outside to catch me anywhere near here. Does he come in here to eat lunch?"

"Naw. He's only been coming in later in the day to fill his coffee thermos," he said. "Free of charge."

"Good, then we have some time to talk. I need to know more about Doris. What did she look like? Do you have a picture of her?"

Carl frowned at me. "Only one, a Polaroid of all of us here. It was taken after closing one night last year when we had a birthday party for one of the girls. You can't see Doris very well, but you can have it if it'll help. Will I get it back?"

I patted his hand. "I'll guard it with my life."

Carl got up and went back into the kitchen and then returned with the photograph. It had a tiny hole in it at the top, as if it had been tacked up on the wall. He handed it to me and pointed out Doris. It was a group picture, taken from across the room. Her features were not clear. She was a blonde, of medium height, but I couldn't discern much else.

"What color eyes did she have?"

"Brown."

"Did she have any distinguishing characteristics or traits, Carl?"

"Like what?"

"I don't know—scars or tattoos or nervous habits. Was there anything unusual about her at all?"

"No. Just the way she talked, like I told you. She always sounded smart, like you—big words. I can't think of anything else."

"What would she say? Can you think of anything typical?"

"She said 'clearly' a lot."

"'Clearly?'"

"Yeah like 'Clearly you can see my point. And one time she said it was 'incumbent' upon me to redecorate the cafe to attract a better class of customers."

I laughed.

"What's so funny?" Carl asked in a tough-guy tone.

"I just … I'm sorry. I just see some humor in your remembering certain words."

"You asked. Anyhow, I did go home and look them up," he said, ducking his head.

"I get the picture. I just wish there was something more, something that would give me a clue at where to start."

"Why don't you talk to the girls? There's time before the lunch rush. Maybe they noticed somethin' I didn't."

"Okay." I was praying for a miracle.

Carl beckoned at the girls and they came over, pulling up chairs around the booth. The three of them were all dressed alike, the same as the previous day, except the uniforms were now blue. They had typical southern names: Mary Sue, Betty Lou and Carol Ann. I was impressed. And envious.

Betty Lou was snide. She immediately pointed out that Doris' hair was not really blond, that Doris touched up the roots monthly. I didn't like her, but the information was helpful. Mary Sue and Carol Ann didn't have much to say. Doris hadn't made close friends of any of them, but had been nice in a standoffish kind of way. Mary Sue said Doris was a good listener, that she let them cry on her shoulder, but never confided her problems in them.

When they'd gone back to their side of the room, I asked Carl what Doris did on her days off.

"Day off. She always worked six days a week with Mondays off."

"What did she do on Mondays? What did she do this past Monday? That was the night she was killed, wasn't it?"

"Yeah. Last Monday she went somewheres and came back around six and ate dinner with me. Afterwards she went back upstairs and I never saw her again until I found her body on Tuesday morning."

"Where did she go?"

"I don't know. She always went somewheres. Every week. Shopping, I guess."

"Did she own a car?"

"Nope. She'd take the bus. Or sometimes she'd borrow my car, but not too much. The bus comes by a couple of blocks from here, and she'd walk over and catch it."

"Where does that bus go?"

"Downtown, but she could get transfers and go anywhere in Houston she wanted. There's even a bus down to Galveston a couple'a times each day. I know 'cause my sister catches it sometimes to go down there to see one of my brothers. She could be going anywhere, Mavis. She never told me."

"Well, would she come home with anything? Groceries or clothes or anything?"

"Sometimes, but there's a grocery store not far from here. She'd go there and pick up things every now and then during the day between lunches and dinners if she was working split shift. She couldn't have needed much. I let 'em eat two meals here."

"You don't have any idea where she'd go on Mondays?"

"I told you, no. Sorry. She kept it to herself," Carl said, shrugging.

"Where did she bank?"

"I don't think she did. I'd cash her checks for her."

"Did she have any credit cards? Did her mail come here to the cafe?"

"She never got any mail. The mailman would have delivered it here if she got any. She never even asked if there was any for her. I thought that was strange—that she didn't get any—but she didn't. I don't guess she had any credit cards because they would've had to send her a bill, but she never got any."

I lit a cigarette and, while I puffed on it, studied a spot on the ceiling for a minute. "What about utility bills or a telephone bill?"

"The utilities are included in the rent, and she didn't have no, I mean, any, telephone. She could have used the one in here if she wanted to, but she never did except when I'd ask her to call one of the girls for me if they were late or something."

"What did she do with her money?"

"I don't know. The pay isn't that great, but the way she lived she could have saved a bundle. She made better tips than the other girls most days and I don't charge a lot of rent for the apartment. Maybe she has some money stashed somewheres."

"I'll look for it while I'm up there. Could she have had a post office box somewhere?"

"Sure, but if she did, I didn't know about it."

"Didn't she carry any keys?"

"Yeah," he perked up, his eyes widening as they looked into mine. "Come to think of it, she used to have a key ring with a key to this place, one to each door upstairs, and a couple of little funny-looking keys on it. I remember because one time right after she started working for me, she laid them on the counter after closing when she was counting her tips. When she caught me lookin', she snatched them up and stuffed them in her pocket. The next time, it was just the three keys I knew about."

"Now we're getting somewhere. I hope the cops didn't find them. Let's go on upstairs, okay?"

Chapter 8

I **WAS AS EXCITED AS A GIRL** on her first car date. If I could just find Doris' keys, I might have a lead. It was a slim chance, but better than anything I'd been able to come up with so far. Carl let me in the back door, which was at the top of a rickety set of stairs in the alley. He went back to the cafe.

I found myself in Doris Jones's kitchen. It was small, with a little, white enamel table and two chairs under the window that overlooked the alley. There were an apartment-sized stove and refrigerator, and a few cabinets around the sink. I pulled open the cabinets. They were filled with resale junk. She had a coffeepot set up on one of the counters and a couple of dish towels in a drawer. It could have been anyone's kitchen.

The table was sort of half set. Placemats and napkins were in front of each chair. To the side was a small plastic bowl filled with pink envelopes of artificial sweetener, and a set of salt and pepper shakers was over to one side of a napkin holder.

The bottom drawer of the stove held the pots and pans. Next to the stove were a mop, a broom, and a two-step kitchen stool with a red plastic seat cover.

The refrigerator was almost empty. The freezer compartment was the same.

I checked out the bathroom. The towels were J.C. Penney. The gaily-striped shower curtain matched the bath mat and toilet cover. Her medicine chest held no prescription drugs.

Her living room was furnished with cheap, plastic-covered furniture except for one comfortable-looking recliner that could have been purchased new. It was still in excellent condition. She had a thirteen-inch color television that sat on a homemade bookshelf of green, yellow, red, and blue one-by-ten boards and cinder blocks.

I took a moment to glance at some of the titles of the paperbacks that adorned the shelves. There was a fair representation of recent best-sellers, but nothing unusual.

I abandoned the living room and went into the bedroom in search of Doris' purse. I was mildly surprised at what I found. The bedroom was her haven, I guess, because it was obvious she'd spent some of her hard-earned money decorating it. There was a nineteen-inch RCA color TV on a metal stand. The furnishings matched, the curtains and bedclothes matched, and the floor was carpeted. The floors of the other rooms were cheap tile squares and wood.

Looking through her chest of drawers, I was again surprised. Her undergarments were Lily of France and Vanity Fair—not inexpensive. She had a drawer full of sweaters and a couple looked like cashmere, but the labels were cut off.

I searched her closet and found several expensive-looking suits. Again no labels. Her blouses were the same, no labels. I knew she couldn't hide the labels in her shoes and when I pulled them off the rack and looked, it was just as I thought—she'd had money at one time or another. The problem was that these days her make of shoes could be found in expensive stores in any large city.

I have to admit it. I was horribly, morbidly curious about Doris Jones. I began to wonder whether that was, in fact, her real name. If she'd gone to all this trouble to hide her past, she had probably changed her name. Besides, a woman like her isn't named Doris or Jones. It was more likely that her first name would be Ashley or Roxanne. I couldn't begin to imagine her last name.

After having a good look around, I went over and sat on the edge of her bed. It was quite possible that the police had confiscated her purse and any papers she had. Most women carried purses, but I didn't find one. I attempted to think like Doris Jones. If I had no bank account, no credit cards, no identification, would I carry a purse? Maybe not. I might carry my money and keys in a pocket and not be bothered.

I went back to the small closet, pulled a shoe box from the top shelf, and opened it. Empty, except for the gray paper that came with the shoes. I grabbed a second one. Bingo. A purse. I quickly opened it, but it was empty. Not even a scrap of paper or a book of matches. I searched two more boxes, but they, too, were empty. Beginning at one end of the closet and working my way through to the other, I explored the pockets of all her clothes. There was nothing, not even in her winter coat or parka.

I left the closet, went over to her bed, and raised up her mattress. You never know. But there wasn't anything there. I examined the drawers of her bedside table, and although I found a small jar of change, that was all. I was growing frustrated. I knew there was literally a key to Doris Jones somewhere in that apartment. Why couldn't I find it? I was convinced that the hiding place would be so easy that any idiot could find it. Why couldn't I? I figured that when she was ready to go wherever it was she went, she wouldn't have to bother to dismantle anything, so her hiding place would be simple.

I went back into the living room and sat in her chair. I'd pretend to be her. If I was going to hide money or a set of keys where it wouldn't be obvious but would be easy to get to, where would I put it? I looked around the room. Books, TV, rug on floor, draperies on windows, sofa, chair, lamp, end table. Having made the full circle of the room, my eyes rested on the books again.

I went over to the bookshelf and pulled a book out at random. I took it by the covers and shook it. Out flew a dollar bill. I shook it again. Another fell out. I grabbed another book and fanned the pages. There were bills here and there. I'd found where she kept her money.

One by one I yanked the books off the shelves and looked in the bindings for a key. I came up empty-handed. I knew that she'd hide the key or keys someplace obvious, and suddenly I knew where. I went back into her bedroom and pulled open the drawer where the jar of change was. I emptied the change out on her bed. There, in the middle of a pile of nickles, dimes, and quarters, was a solitary key.

It was small with strange teeth, but I recognized it as a safe deposit box key. My year as a bank teller when I was in college had paid off. Part of that job was relieving the lady who was in charge of safe deposit boxes.

The problem now was, what bank? There must be a million banks doing business in Houston, Texas. How was I going to figure out in which bank Doris Jones had hidden something? And if I did figure it out, how would I get into her box? The thought of going to the police with what I'd found never even entered my mind.

I scooped up the change and returned it to the jar, the jar to the drawer, and sat down to think again, staring at the key resting in the palm of my hand.

A sense of hopelessness was beginning to overtake me. I was hot and tired and the apartment air was smelly and stifling I couldn't turn on the window air-conditioning unit without giving myself away. Forcing myself to get up, I began searching again.

I opened a small jewelry box that I found on the dresser, but it was filled with costume jewelry and a single tiny gold chain. I was expecting to find something more valuable. Another box contained some scarves and some thin grosgrain ribbons that were knotted at each end.

I went back to the closet to examine her wardrobe a little more closely on the off chance that maybe she had forgotten something. I scrutinized each item of clothing meticulously. I pulled each sweater down from the shelf and searched it. When the shelf was seemingly bare, I got the kitchen step stool and returned to the closet. Standing on the stool, I examined the surface of the shelf. I was hoping for a clothing receipt, a tag, a label, something taped down to the shelf, anything. But there was nothing. She had covered herself like a pro.

Stepping down, I sat on the stool and faced the interior of the closet, staring, trying to come up with an ingenious idea. I noticed that the left-hand side of the ceiling of the closet contained an access door to the attic crawl space.

I got down off the stool and moved it so that I could reach that side of the closet ceiling. I climbed up, my hands shaking with excitement, and reached up over my head. With a gentle shove, the trapdoor moved easily to one side. I climbed a step higher, which is no easy feat for me since I suffer from acrophobia, and clung to the frame of the opening as I stuck a hand inside.

It was dark up there, and the space was not very large. It would have been possible only to crawl, which is why it has the name it does, I guess, but I can't imagine anyone wanting to do so. I groped around, searching for something, anything, so long as it wasn't furry and didn't move. And I found what I was looking for.

I grasped the shoe box, pulled it down with me, and hurried back over to the bed. Removing the top, I found a self carbon of a receipt for a safe deposit box at Dickinson State Bank. It was dated the preceding Monday and had a hand-written notation that said "renewal rent." Doris Jones's signature was scrawled across the bottom. Needless to say, I was elated.

Under the receipt was a letter, but no envelope. It was dated two weeks ago.

Dear Mother,

I miss you so much lately that I can hardly stand it. I think about you all the time and wonder what it would be like if you were here to go shopping with me and help me pick out my prom dress.

Why haven't you called recently? I miss talking to you. There is something I need to tell you but I don't know how to do it in a letter. It's about Dad.

Anne misses you, too. Every once in a while she talks about how she misses your loud mouth cheering for her at the ball games. Ha ha.

Seriously, she is getting so good that her coach says she may make the All-Star team this year. I know she'd like it if you would come home and see her play. Also there's this boy she likes that calls her all the time. You wouldn't believe how pretty she is when she's dressed up.

Mom, is there any possibility that you could come home for my graduation? Will your "problem" be solved by then? I hope so.

Please call me at the usual time and place next week. I'll be waiting by the phone. It's really important. Don't forget.

I love you and wish you were here.

Love, Catherine

I read the letter twice before I could look further into Doris' shoe box. My eyes blurred at the thought of this lady who had left her husband and two children and was hiding out because of some "problem." It must have been really horrible for her to have left them.

I laid the letter in my lap and reached for the next one. When I lifted it out of the box, the only item left was a family photograph, the faces staring up at me. There was a man, a woman, and two girls. The man appeared to be in his thirties. He had almost-blond hair, and blue eyes, and wore glasses. He looked very nice. The older of the two girls was standing behind the younger. The younger looked like she was around twelve or thirteen while the older looked closer to sixteen or seventeen. Between the younger girl and the man was a lady with brown hair and brown eyes, and a pleasant, oval-shaped face. She wore a single strand of pearls around her neck and a soft-looking, blue blouse.

I read the other letter. It was brief and to the point and dated the previous week.

Dear Mother,

Why haven't I heard from you? I've been by the phone when I'm supposed to. Please call me at the usual time when you get this.

It's real, real important! About Madge!

Love, Catherine

I gathered up the letters, the receipt, and the picture, and put them in my shoulder bag. I didn't want to show them to Carl just yet. I glanced at my watch. It had been two hours since my arrival. It was past time to go before Lon Tyler would remember the woman in curlers had gone into, but had never come out of, the cafe.

I hurriedly straightened up the mess I'd made in the closet, replaced the stool in the kitchen, gathered up the money I'd left lying on the floor of the living room and stuffed it back into the books, and stuffed the books on the shelves. Once I satisfied myself that everything looked the way it had when I arrived, I let myself out the back door.

When I went back through the cafe kitchen, Carl was busy cooking. It was the end of the lunch-time rush, which gave me a good excuse not to stop and talk. I smiled at Carl and told him I'd call him later. Then I headed for the door.

I was just approaching the front of the cafe and slipping on my crazy sunglasses when the door was pushed open in front of me. I was suddenly face-to-face with Lon Tyler, who was packing a large thermos under one arm. I'm afraid I almost panicked, I was so surprised, but my glasses were by then upon my nose and when he uttered, "'S'cuse me," I merely murmured my assent and slipped out the door.

My hands and knees were shaking as I pulled the door closed and let the screen door slam shut behind me. I had to restrain myself from running all the way back to my car.

Really, I scolded myself, if I was going to be a detective I was going to have to learn to keep my cool. When I reached my car I drove as fast as possible out of the neighborhood. The devil himself would have had a hard time catching me.

Chapter 9

MAVIS DAVIS PRODUCTIONS," MARGARET APPLEBAUM'S **HIGH-PITCHED** voice sang into the phone when I called her from my apartment after I got out of the shower.

"Hey Margaret, it's me," I said.

"Hi, Mavis. Where've you been? You won't believe the calls we've been getting to serve papers."

"When it rains, it pours. Listen, I've been over to Doris Jones's apartment and found a bank where she has a safe deposit box. I need you to call and see if she had an account there, okay?"

"Sure, Mavis, but what if they won't tell me?"

"No, Margaret, what you do is you don't ask them if she had an account, you call and say that you are verifying her account with that bank before you approve her credit. You state that she's trying to purchase something from your company."

"What company?"

"Make it up, Margaret," I said tersely.

"Well, what would she be buying?"

"A TV or something." Sigh. "You say that she stated on her credit application that she had an account there. Call the bookkeeping department. You just want to verify that she indeed has a checking or savings account before your company opens a charge account."

"Oh. Okay. What's the name of the bank?" Margaret asked.

"Dickinson State Bank."

"Where's that?"

It's a good thing I was not at the office. I swear I would have turned violent. "Dickinson," I answered. "Remember the little city on the bayou about thirty minutes from here where they have the Strawberry Festival every spring? Call Information for the number or dig through that stack of phone books that's stored in the cabinet in the bathroom."

"Is that all you want me to do?"

"Yeah, for now. Has Candy gotten there yet?"

"No. Remember she had to go to the library today to finish a research paper? She's gonna be late. You want me to lock up and go pick up those papers to serve?"

I had a plan, but I wasn't going to let Margaret in on it yet. I was afraid she'd panic. I needed her to go to the bank with me, but until I could talk to her in person to keep her calm, my lips had to remain sealed.

"Tell you what, Margaret, call those people back and find out where the people they want served are located. We'll do service on anyone south of the courthouse, 'cause we're heading that way this afternoon. We'll just have to pass on the rest of them. Suggest someone else to do the others."

"What's going on, Mavis?"

"Tell you when I get there. Go ahead and call those people and pick up the service on the ones I said, and meet me back at the office a.s.a.p. Okay? Just be sure you call that bank before you do anything else."

"Right, Mavis. I wrote it all down. Want me to read it back to you?"

"No. I trust you, Margaret." I rolled my eyes toward the ceiling, but luckily she couldn't see me.

"Okay, Mavis. See you in a little while."

I hung up the phone. Once more I was questioning my sanity regarding hiring Margaret. I had known her for years. In fact, we went through high school together and had been good buddies. I had worked and gone on to college, and she, to business school. When I opened my office, she applied for the job as sort of a girl Friday, which is what I needed. She was perfect for office work—a whiz at the computer and other business machines. The trouble seemed to be that she had been shorted on day-to-day, good-old-fashioned common sense. But she was a dear. It was hard not to like her. And she was true blue. I just had to learn patience.

I dried my hair and got into suitable clothes and drove out to the office where I waited for Margaret to return with the citations and subpoenas that we were to serve. By the time she arrived, Candy had also shown up. We started with a brief powwow so that I could bring them up to date, and I told Candy about the safe deposit box.

"So now you gotta get into her box, huh?" Candy asked. Candy had a lot of brains. I figured that one of these days she was going to become normal. Well, as normal as any of the rest of us, with one-color hair, two earrings at a time, regular solid-colored button-down-collar shirts, and plain blue jeans.

"Right, Candy. My guess is that Doris was hiding something in that box that is crucial to her identity or else that's crucial to the reason why she was hiding."

Margaret was nodding her head in agreement by this time. She was propped up at the computer as if she had made the assumption that I was going to dictate the solution to the case for her so that she could add it to our notes of yesterday. Candy was snapping her gum, six earrings dangling as she leaned up against the counter.

"How're you going to get into the box, Mavis?" Margaret asked. I could see her watching my reflection in the monitor of the computer. Hopefully she didn't catch my wink at Candy.

"Did she have an account at that bank, Margaret?" I asked without replying to her query.

"Oh no. No checking, no savings, no certificates of deposit, so then I even told them we couldn't approve her for credit."

"Good. That's what I suspected. No connection with that bank except for her safe deposit box. That means that a minimal number of people have ever seen Doris Jones, right?"

The girls nodded, both sets of eyes questioning.

I pulled out the photograph of the group at The Rex and held it out for them to see, pointing to Doris. "That was Doris Jones."

"Oh, I see," said Candy, "the one with the blond hair." She grinned conspiratorially at me and indicated Margaret with a jerk of her head.

"Right," I said aloud. Margaret still didn't seem to have caught on. "And here is the receipt she just got for renewing the rent on the box." I showed both girls the receipt I had concealed in my pocket. "See her signature, Margaret?" I asked, smiling my sincerest and warmest smile.

"Yes, I see it, Mavis," Margaret answered. "So what about it?"

"Think you can learn it in less than twenty-four hours?"

Margaret's eyes grew quite large. "You mean you want me to forge Doris Jones's signature at the bank?"

Candy's eyes were dancing. I knew she would have gladly done it, but she had the wrong color hair. Besides, she was too young.

"Fortune smiled upon us, Margaret Applebaum, when you decided to bleach your hair blond. For in doing so, you became the perfect candidate to enter Doris Jones's safe deposit box and retrieve the solution to the Mystery of Doris Jones." I had pulled up a chair opposite of and to the side of Margaret and was staring into her eyes with the most pitiful look possible on my little freckled face.

"No. Oh, no, Mavis, that's not part of my job description. I'm not going to jail for you," Margaret said, shaking her head back and forth nonstop.

"Without you, two young girls may never know their mother is dead, Margaret. Without you, somewhere a husband will wonder forever what happened to his wife. Without you, Mr. Singleton will probably not give us any more money and Candy may be out of a job."

"What?" Candy nearly shouted from where she stood on the other side of Margaret.

"We've been running pretty low on money lately, Candy," I said sympathetically as I shrugged my shoulders. "With this case, our present financial problems would have been solved. But without it—well I'm sorry. Things are tough all over."

"Aw, Mavis, I need this job. I was counting on working here all summer. I haven't even applied anywhere else." Candy was beginning the whine that was one of her most deplorable traits. I had been working on it with her, and she had been progressing. I don't suppose I could blame her now though.

During this exchange, Margaret was sitting in her chair facing the monitor, a dazed expression on her face. Suddenly she said, "What two young girls?"

I grew excited. I had her hooked. I hoped. I pulled the second picture from my purse and flashed it at them. "This is Doris Jones with her family," I said, confident that I was correct. "And I imagine that Doris Jones is not her real name." I gave the photograph to Margaret to hold. Next I got out the letters and unfolded them. "Here, Margaret, read these letters from Doris' daughter." I gave them to Margaret to read while I paced the floor. That was all my ammunition. If Margaret refused, I was in big trouble. The thought of bleaching my own hair had crossed my mind, and it was not pleasing to me

Candy was standing behind Margaret, reading over her shoulder. After a short period of time, I heard one of them sniff. I'm not sure which one. I was silent, awaiting Margaret's answer. "Okay, Mavis," Margaret said softly. "What's your plan?" I skipped back to her side of the room, grabbed her by the shoulders, and hugged her with all my might.

"You're a pal, Margaret," I said. "Now, this is what we do. We go out to the bank this afternoon and case it to see if we can figure out who the regular lady is that works in safe deposit boxes. Then tomorrow, when she goes to lunch, you enter the bank and approach her substitute. You'll have Doris' key and ask to get into your safe deposit box. You'll sign Doris' signature on the card that the lady presents to you and go in and remove everything that is in the box."

Margaret looked worried. "Gee, I don't know, Mavis. Suppose they've read the Houston paper and know that Doris has been murdered?"

"C'mon, Margaret, how many Doris Jones's do you suppose are in this world? There's probably a hundred of them in Houston alone. Besides, there wasn't any picture, and the police don't know about this box so they wouldn't have told the bank. Don't worry about it."

"Easy for you to say," Margaret said.

I just stared at her imploringly.

"Well, what if the regular lady takes her lunch and eats at her desk? Or what if she remembers me from today when we go in there?" Margaret asked.

Candy and I exchanged glances. Margaret was resisting and we had to bolster her courage.

Candy spoke up. "Mavis and I will go in there together today, Margaret, and we'll go to new accounts or something and ask about their rates on CDs or something. You can stay in the car. Mavis and I will scope out the joint. Then tomorrow we'll go in there separately, and when we've seen that the regular lady isn't there, we'll come out and tell you."

"No, we won't," I said.

Candy stared. "Why not? I thought that was a good idea," she said with a touch of whine again.

"We'll go in there this afternoon, Candy, but I'll go in there by myself tomorrow. You'll still be in school when we have to leave to get down for lunchtime."

"Aw c'mon, Mavis. I was gonna cut class."

"No way. They're not going to get me for contributing to the delinquency of a minor," I remarked with a shake of my head.

"You're asking Margaret to forge a signature and steal the contents of a safe deposit box, and you're worried about a little contributing charge?"

"Yeah," Margaret said.

"Look. I'm not jeopardizing Candy's status at school. Besides, I don't want Candy to be a part of all this. We shouldn't even be discussing this in front of her, Margaret. She's just a child."

"Heavier shit than this comes down on the street in my neighborhood," Candy said with a huge pout on her face.

"Well, you're not getting out of school," I said, ignoring her epithet.

"I don't care what you say. Margaret and I are supposed to be setting an example for you."

"Aw, that's not fair," Candy whined. "You two get to have all the fun."

"Like it or lump it, I'm not changing my mind. You can help today or you can stay here. Regardless of which you decide, we've got to get a move on before the bank closes this afternoon."

"You know what, Mavis?" Margaret addressed me timidly. She wasn't used to my being so firm about things.

"What?"

"I shouldn't go this afternoon. I mean, it's not that I don't want to, but I shouldn't even be seen in the car with you and Candy. Why don't I stay here and answer the phone and practice Doris' signature and you and Candy can go look at the bank and serve the papers."

"You're not going to chicken out on me tomorrow, are you?" I asked with my most intense look.

"No. Really. Think about it. It only makes sense that we don't want to attract a lot of attention today," Margaret said.

"Like, she's right, you know, Mavis?" Candy said. "Let's go. We'll get an idea of the layout and we can tell her all about it when we get back."

"We do attract a lot of attention when we're all together," I said. "Okay. Candy, get whatever you need. Margaret, you surprise me sometimes. Give me the papers."

Candy went toward the kitchen.

"Thanks, Mavis," Margaret said with a little smile. "There's only three of them. Two subpoenas and one citation." She grabbed a handful of folded-up papers off one of the desks and gave them to me. "I'll study her signature real carefully, Mavis. I'm sure I can imitate it. Remember how I used to sign our mothers' names to excuses when we skipped school?"

"Shh. Not so loud. We really do have to be better about setting an example for Candy, Margaret," I said and grinned at the memory.

Margaret got up from where she sat and came over to me. "I'm scared, Mavis. What if I get caught?" She had a worried expression on her face.

I couldn't answer her right away. I was scared, too. This was making me more nervous than the time I paid a home visit on one of my probationers and a huge, barking, German shepherd came outside to greet me. I smiled and patted Margaret's arm.

"It'll be all right," was all I could manage.

"Ready, Mavis," Candy called as she yanked open the front door and the bell clanked.

"See ya later," I said over my shoulder to Margaret as I grabbed my shoulder bag and headed for the door. I couldn't stand any more discussion about it. We just had to do it and that's all there was to it. Necessity was the mother of invention and all that.

Candy insisted that we put the top down on my Mustang since the air-conditioning wasn't working very well, so a few minutes later we were whizzing down Interstate 45 toward Dickinson, our hair flying in the wind. We planned to scope out the bank first, as Candy would say, and then get to serving the papers.

I swear when we entered the bank I felt like one-half of Bonnie and Clyde. If I recall, they used to run around in Texas, but I don't think there was even a Dickinson back then, much less a Dickinson State Bank.

We went over to the new accounts desk and pretended that Candy was my daughter and was thinking of opening her first checking account. We had a nice chat with the girl there. She was pleasant enough, a brunette with dimples in her cheeks and a friendly smile. We asked her to point out all the services that the bank had to offer. She did so, including the safe deposit box area.

I went into a little more depth with the young lady while Candy pretended to get bored and wander around the bank. I asked about their rates on individual retirement accounts and certificates of deposit. We talked about treasury bills and the latest movement of interest rates.

Eventually, Candy returned and winked at me. We left, much to the enormous relief of everyone, I'm sure, including me, and on my way out I stole a look at the lady at the desk at the back of the bank. Now if it would only be that easy the next day.

Chapter 10

LATE FRIDAY MORNING, MARGARET AND I headed back down the Gulf Freeway. Candy and I had briefed Margaret on what we'd found, and Margaret's forgery of Doris Jones's signature was excellent. There was no reason not to move forward although I'm sure Margaret was racking her brain to come up with one.

Rather than take a chance on things being a little different from what Doris would have done, I had taken the time the previous day to find the bus stop. That's where I let Margaret out, and where I would meet her when she returned.

I drove to the bank parking lot, parked, went inside to see if the regular lady was gone, crossed through the bank to the door on the other side, and returned to Margaret to give her the go-ahead.

I sat near the bus stop and watched Margaret until she disappeared, and then I waited with what had to be bated breath for her to reappear.

What seemed like one-hundred-years later, I saw Margaret walking toward me. As she grew closer, I saw that her face was very white. She reached the car, got in, and to my "Well?" she only said, "Let's go."

I drove west toward the freeway for a few minutes, waiting for Margaret to break the silence. I was watching her more than the road. She was trembling all over like a person who was recovering from a severe shock. Suddenly she spoke.

"Pull over," she demanded.

"What?" I asked, puzzled.

"Pull over to the side of the road," she ordered in a loud voice.

I complied.

Margaret jerked the car door open, leaned out, and threw up all over the pavement. When she was quite finished, she pulled herself together, closed the door, and smiled weakly at me.

"That's better," she said, wiping at her mouth with a tissue.

"Are you okay?" I asked. I'd never known Margaret to be sickly.

"Yes, just nerves. But Mavis, it was the most exciting thing I've ever done in my life!"

She laughed then and held out a fist toward me. It was the first I noticed that her hand was clenching something.

I reached out and opened my palm to take whatever it was she was offering. Into my hand fell three golden rings.

One was a wedding band over a quarter of an inch wide; one was a diamond solitaire; the third was a school ring. My hands shook with excitement.

"We've got to talk about this, Margaret," I said, handing back the rings. "Let's drive up to the next exit and get something to eat someplace where it's cool." I pulled back onto the road and headed toward the interstate.

"How can you eat at a time like this?"

"My oral fixation. Tell me what school that one ring is from," I said.

Margaret looked closely at the ring. "It says J.D., University of Texas School of Law."

"Wow! A lawyer! Is it a woman's ring? Try it on. See if it fits."

Margaret slipped it on the ring finger of her right hand. I almost ran off the road trying to watch what she was doing. It wouldn't go over the knuckle.

"I'll bet it's a pinkie ring," said Margaret as she slipped it off her ring finger and onto her pinkie. "It is. It almost fits me. Mavis, Doris was a lawyer."

"God—can you imagine?" I'm afraid I chortled.

"It must have been something really terrible for a woman lawyer to run off and leave her husband and kids and her profession," Margaret said. She stared down at the ring on her little finger, stroking it with the thumb of her left hand.

We both got quiet for a few minutes while we thought of our find. By that time we were approaching the League City exit. I got off and crossed over the freeway and drove to McDonald's, where we went for hamburgers. Margaret brought the rings inside with her.

We sat in a booth next to a window and examined the rings.

"Look inside the law school ring and see if there is an inscription," I instructed Margaret.

She peered at the inside of the ring. "Yes, E.A.R. and then it says 14K."

"So her name wasn't Doris," I said. "I didn't think so. Let's look at the others. May I see the wedding ring?"

Margaret handed me the wedding band and I looked at the inside of it. It read, "Robert to Elizabeth 6-15-70."

"Elizabeth R.," Margaret whispered in a breathless tone.

"I knew her name would be something like that," I said. "Her daughters are Catherine and Anne."

"I'll bet the middle initial is for Anne," Margaret said.

"You're probably right." Margaret looked pleased with herself. "So her name was Elizabeth Anne R. something. We can probably figure out who she was by going to the law school. Does that ring have a year on it?"

Margaret scrutinized the ring. "No, just a Latin phrase and the letters J.D. and University of Texas School of Law. What's J.D.?"

"Juris Doctorate." She handed it to me and I looked it over. It had a set of longhorns on one side and a capital U with a capital T over it on the other. She was right, no year. We still didn't know who Doris really was, but we were a lot closer than we had been a few hours before. It suddenly occurred to me that Margaret hadn't told me what else she had found in the box.

"What else was there, Margaret?"

"That's it." She held her palms up, indicating. "It was weird, you know,

Mavis? It was a large box, about a foot wide and real deep, but nothing else was in it. Don't they have smaller boxes than that?"

"Yeah, most banks have several sizes. The size you're describing sounds like the second smallest, about the size that people get for storing their coin collections and legal and insurance papers."

"I wonder what else she could have gotten it for?"

"I don't know, Margaret, but we need to keep that question in mind. Could you tell how many times she'd gone into it?"

"No. The lady took an index card and covered up everything so I could only see the line I was signing on—I couldn't even see Doris' name typed at the top. Then she held the card down on the desk and told me to sign. And then, when I finished, she stared at the card real hard and then at me for a minute before taking me into the vault. I just knew I'd been caught. I was so scared." Her eyes grew wide as she recited. Then she laughed.

"No wonder you threw up," I said. "Well, I guess at this point we'd better talk to Carl and see whether he wants us to proceed. The thought's occurred to me that when I tell him Doris, I mean Elizabeth, was married, that he might want to call it quits."

"I'd hate that, Mavis. I'm so curious now that I could burst."

"Me, too, but unfortunately we can't proceed on our own. We can't afford it. The best we could do would be to turn over what we've found to the police and hope they'd do something with it."

"Then we'd really be in trouble," Margaret said.

"Yeah. Let's pray that Carl is as curious as we are."

Chapter 11

A T ONE O'CLOCK ON FRIDAY AFTERNOON, Margaret Applebaum and I pulled up parallel to Lon Tyler, waved in his face, and parked in front of him across from The Rex. I couldn't believe he was still there. I mean, what was the point? Did he think someone was going to get nervous, run over to him, lean in the car window, and confess?

We crossed the street and went inside the café, into the lovely air-conditioning, and found an empty table near the kitchen. Carl was busy slapping over-laden plates up into the window, so when Mary Sue came over, Margaret and I ordered diet drinks to sip while we waited until Carl could take a break.

We were in the middle of expounding on a theory when Lon Tyler barged in. He threw open the door; his eyes sought us out; and he marched directly to our table.

Hovering over us like a vulture, he glared down at me while sizing up Margaret. The armpits of his rumpled brown suit—yes, his suit—were stained, as was the mismatched tie that hung loosely around his fat neck. "The Captain says I should talk to you," he grumbled.

"How sweet," I replied, deliberately not inviting him to sit down.

"Who's this?" he asked, indicating Margaret with a jerk of his head.

"My assistant, Margaret Applebaum. Margaret, this is Lon Tyler of the Houston Police Department. Homicide Division, I believe."

Margaret held out her hand, as any polite, modern, young woman would do, but Lon didn't take it. I'm sure she was relieved.

"Sergeant Tyler," he muttered, still standing there staring down with his beady little bird eyes.

I wasn't impressed, and I could tell from her expression that Margaret wasn't either. We stayed there, looking at each other, until it dawned on me that Lon wasn't going away. Neither was he going to talk in front of Margaret. "Margaret," I said, "go play the juke box." I felt like I was talking to a child.

Margaret smiled wanly, snatched her purse off the table, and slid out of the booth. Clearly, she was insulted.

Tyler slid his bulk in, bumped the table, and almost caused my soda to spill over. As it was, I had to catch the plastic flowers before they hit the floor. Leaning his elbows rudely on the table, he scowled at me. Once again, my nose was offended by the result of his having sat outside during the heat of the day. I leaned back into the bench seat, but could only get just so far from him. I smiled, probably wanly, too.

"What can I do for you, Sergeant Tyler?"

"Didn't Sergeant Sorensen talk to you?" he asked gruffly as he pointed his stubby forefinger in my face.

Before I answered, I pulled out a pack of cigarettes, shook one out, and flicked my lighter, gazing at him through the butane flame. After I inhaled deeply, I exhaled right into his face. "Why, yes. We had dinner together the other night," I said sweetly, as if passing the time of day. "I had a nice—"

"I don't care what you had," he growled. "Didn't he tell you to leave the Jones case alone? Didn't he? What are you doing here? Huh?"

"Why Lon, Margaret and I stopped by here to get soft drinks. It's awfully hot outside and we were thirsty. Can't you see?" I said, indicating our drinks. "I thought I'd talk to Mr. Singleton again about the apartment. I'm still interested."

"Bullshit," he said with an offensive tone in his voice. If it was possible, his face was getting redder than it had been when he came in out of the heat.

At that point, I didn't know if I should fess up or not. How much secrecy did Carl want? I had little inclination to give away what we'd discovered, especially in light of Margaret's participation. And then there was Candy to consider. She was going to be awfully upset if I got into trouble and she didn't have a job anymore. I'm afraid I just sat there waiting to see what would happen if I was simply nonresponsive.

"Did Singleton hire you?"

"For what?"

"For anything?"

"I hesitate to breach any confidentiality."

"You want to go downtown with me?"

"Hey, that's great, Lon. Just like they say it in the movies."

"You're going to be in big trouble if you don't answer my questions."

"Here," I held out my hands toward him, wrists together, "cuff me. Arrest me. Take me downtown. But first tell me what law I've broken by coming in here to buy a Coke."

"It ain't the Coke. It's the looking into the Jones murder that's got you into trouble, and you know it."

"Tell me one thing that I've done wrong."

"No license."

"Hah! Got you there! I got my license two months ago. Besides, where does it say that I have to have a license to talk to a friend about his bereavement?"

"See! You've admitted it! You are looking into the Jones murder."

"I said no such thing."

"You'd better tell me what you know."

"About what? I know a lot of things."

I was watching Lon's face during this exchange. It wasn't a pleasant sight. The veins at his temples turned blue and bulged as though they were going to burst. He had a mean, stressed-out look around his bloodshot eyes. His nostrils were flaring. The muscles in his jaws were flexing. His lips formed a grim, thin line. I began to wonder how far I could push my luck.

"Look, Mavis," Lon finally said tiredly, putting on his "broken man" act. "I'm just trying to do my job, ya' know? I been sitting out there for four days watching this place, and you're the only hope I got to get relieved of this job. Now will you tell me what you know so that maybe the captain will let me go back to regular duty?"

My heart didn't go out to him. I sat there, close mouthed, trying to decide what I could do to get rid of him. The air around us was becoming oppressive. I glanced toward the jukebox, hoping for help from Margaret, but she had her back to me. I was sure she was deliberately refusing to be supportive. I couldn't blame her.

I looked toward the kitchen. Carl was peering through the window, watching us with those sleepy blue eyes of his. He motioned to me, as if to ask whether he should come over. I shook my head just a tad. My eyes came back to rest on Lon, not a pretty sight.

"Turnabout's fair play, y'know, Lon?"

"So?"

"Tit for tat?"

"Okay."

"You go first."

"No," he said, sitting up authoritatively in his seat, "you."

"What the shit," I said with a shrug. "You should have believed Carl when he told you she wasn't part of the serial killings."

"How's that?"

"Doris Jones was not killed by the same person that killed those other two women."

"Get outta here."

"You asked. I'm tellin'. It wasn't a stranger who killed her. It was someone she knew."

"Yeah? And where are you getting your information?"

I shook my head and sighed. I could tell this idea wasn't nifty keen. I was going to come away feeling like a frustrated old maid at a Mother's

Day parade when I got through butting heads with Lon, but there was something I wanted to know and I was sure Lon had the answer. "Look, Lon, are you going to listen to me or what? Read my lips, it wasn't the serial killer. Now I want to know something."

He was shaking his head and rolled his eyes, as if to say he thought he was talking to an idiot. That was okay. I was not insulted. If he got to thinking I wasn't a threat, maybe he'd go away and leave me alone.

"What?"

"Did y'all find any keys?"

"What?" he repeated.

"A key ring. Did the police find a key ring with a set of keys on it?" Boy, was he slow.

"You mean the apartment keys and the key to the cafe?"

"Yeah." I tried to hide my elation. "Is that all there was?"

"What are you getting at?" he asked evasively. He must have sensed my excitement.

"I thought maybe she had another key, like to a mailbox or a safe deposit box."

"What would she want that for? What would a dame like Doris Jones want with a safe deposit box for Christ's sake?"

"To hide something in. To hide her identity in."

"Now I've heard everything," he said, shaking his head at me. "Are you nuts, Mavis?"

"No—really, Lon. I've got this theory that Doris Jones was not Doris Jones, that she was someone else. I think she was hiding out and whoever she was hiding from found her and killed her."

"Jesus Christ, Mavis! Where did you get such a stupid idea?"

"It fits. And if she had such a key, then we could go find out who killed her. Maybe."

Lon chuckled and slapped his hand down on the table. I had to catch the flower vase again. "Well, there ain't no safe deposit box key," he said, mimicking my tone of voice, "and that's the dumbest idea I ever heard of."

I was indignant. At least I hope that's the impression I conveyed. I was trying my damnedest to be the actress my mother always said I was when things didn't go my way. "Well, that's my theory anyway, Lon."

He was laughing loudly now, as if someone had tickled his funny bone. Such huge bellows came out of him that the few remaining lunch customers turned to stare at us. It was great.

I cast my eyes at him, apparently hurt by his laughter, and stubbed my cigarette out in the ashtray. "Okay, Lon. That's enough. If you don't stop, I'm not going to talk about it anymore." I crossed my arms about my chest and pushed my lower lip out.

Lon let go of a couple more guffaws, wiped the tears of laughter from the corners of his eyes, and then he went away. He simply scooted out of the bench seat, bumping the table again as he went, walked up to the counter and got a cup of coffee, and went out the door, turning once or twice to grin at me in the process.

I looked horribly insulted until he was out of sight; then I suppose I looked like the Cheshire cat. Margaret and Carl arrived at the table at the same time.

"What was that all about?" Carl asked as he slid onto the bench seat where Lon had been.

I moved over to make room for Margaret and then shrugged my shoulders. "He didn't appreciate our theory of the case, Carl, that's all. Hopefully it'll keep him off my back."

"He sure was loud," Margaret said.

"I know. I'm sorry," I said to Carl.

"Aw, that's okay, Mavis. Boy, he's really something." Carl said.

"Yeah, and he's probably going to say the same thing about me tonight when he gets back to the station. But that's all right. Listen, Carl, we've got so much to tell you. Are you ready for this?"

Carl swiped at his crew cut, wiped his hands on his grease-stained apron, and then cupped his chin as he rested his elbow on the table. His mouth turned down in a frown as he answered. "Fire when ready."

I glanced at Margaret for courage, because we both knew that Carl might terminate our working relationship when he heard what we'd learned.

Margaret had a stiff-upper-lip expression on her face. The truth had to be told. It was the end of the week and Carl had paid to know the answers to the questions he'd raised.

My eyes cut back to Carl's. "Doris Jones was really Elizabeth something or other. The initials of the rest of her name are A. R. We think her middle name was Anne."

He expelled a breath of air, almost as audible as the bursting of a day-old balloon. His eyes darted from me to Margaret. She nodded in confirmation. Back to me, he said, "Go on."

"We think she was a lawyer."

"I knew it!" He slammed his palm on the table. The surface was getting quite a workout that day.

"Well, you were right." I smiled because he seemed so pleased with himself.

"Did you tell that cop?" he asked.

"He wouldn't have believed me, but no, I didn't."

"How'd you find out?"

"Uh, I'd rather not say," I said with another look in Margaret's direction. "Not just now. But you can believe that we have some evidence to support our contention."

"God, it's amazing how much you sound like her sometimes, Mavis," he said with a grin. "That's just the kind of thing Doris—I mean Elizabeth—would say." He paused a minute and then ran his hand across the back of his neck. "That's strange, thinking about her as Elizabeth, but it's a nice name. It suits her. I mean, it would have—you know what I mean," he ended.

"Yes," Margaret said, "we know."

"But please, you've got to tell me how you know."

Margaret's eyes were taking on a worried expression, her eyebrows knitting together under all that hair. I reached out and patted her arm reassuringly. She had to know I wouldn't betray her.

"Ask me no questions, and I'll tell you no lies," Margaret said.

"Oh okay."

"There's more, Carl, and I'm not sure you're going to like it," I said.

"What is it?"

"She was married and had kids."

He sighed and shrugged his shoulders. "I'm not surprised. A woman like that it would be more of a shock if she didn't have anyone. You would have had to know her." His eyes glazed over just a bit, as if he were remembering something.

We sat and watched him, waiting for the next question. He was almost pitiful, the way he sat there. His stained white chef's apron hung round his neck over his blue work shirt. The working class stiff musing over the professional woman who had always been out of his reach.

"What do you know about them? Him?"

I reached into my purse and pulled out the family portrait and handed it to him. He took it and stared down at the smiling faces in the photograph for a moment and then raised his eyes to mine. "Nice family. She was a nice-looking woman even with brown hair."

"Yes."

"Two girls. I'll bet they're wondering where their mother is," he said hoarsely. "I'll bet he is, too."

It was tough, sitting there like that with Carl. It was almost tragic to see him show concern for her family.

"Catherine, that's the older girl," I said and pointed to her face in the picture, "had been in touch with her mother."

"She had?"

"Yes." I reached back into my bag and pulled out the letters, handing him the long one. Then Margaret and I sat in silence again for a few minutes while he read it. We watched, as he glanced from the letter, to the photograph, to us.

"That's really a tearjerker," he said sincerely.

"Here's another one. It's a lot shorter."

He took the second letter and read through it quickly. "Where were they postmarked?"

"There weren't any envelopes. I don't yet know where they live," I said hesitantly. I never would if he didn't pay us to do any more work. As curious as we were, we couldn't afford to find out if we weren't paid to do so.

"What else?"

"That's about it. We found some rings; that's how we know she was probably an attorney. Show them to him, Margaret." Margaret reached into her purse and then handed the rings over to Carl. He examined them and handed them back. "That diamond's a knockout," he said.

"Yes. They apparently weren't hurting for money. Did you look at the law school ring? The University of Texas was where she went," I said.

"Then you should be able to find out what her real name was," Carl said.

"Yes. If I go to Austin." Mentally, I put on my business cap. "I wanted to talk to you about that. I didn't know if you wanted us to go any further or not. After all, it is Friday."

Much to my relief, Carl said, "You wouldn't quit on me now, would you, Mavis? Could you go to Austin?"

"I'd be glad to if you're willing to pay my expenses and my fee," I said directly. Talking money was very difficult for me, so generally I just blurted it out and waited to get the person's reaction.

"Well, we can't quit now. This is great, Mavis. You're terrific!"

I smiled demurely. I was secretly hoping he'd be pleased.

"Aren't you excited, Mavis?" asked Carl.

I glanced at Margaret and we grinned at each other and then laughed at the same time. "Yeah, it's really neat what we've found. We've practically been in hysterics all morning. We just didn't know how you'd feel."

"We didn't know if you'd be willing to continue once you found out she was married," Margaret said.

"We wanted to proceed, Carl, but business is business. If you didn't care to go any further with the investigation, we didn't know what we could do with it. We couldn't tell the police everything we knew because of some of the means of getting the information. If, in the end, we find out who did it, then maybe there won't be a problem, but right now there would be. Do you understand what I'm trying to say?" I asked.

"Yeah. I can tell that you don't know me very well. When I start something, I finish it. And with Doris, rather Elizabeth, I want to keep on going until I know what happened. You understand me, Mavis? I don't care what it costs. I'll borrow money if I run out. Whoever killed her deserves to be caught and her family deserves to know what happened to her."

"We agree," I said.

"When can you leave for Austin?"

Chapter 12

I LUCKED OUT. I HAVE A FRIEND who's a doctor and lives over near the medical center with her mechanic husband. I called Alex on Saturday morning and begged and pleaded until he agreed to look at my air-conditioner that afternoon. He was able to rig it up temporarily with Freon and a patch, and he also gave me the bad news. For a permanent fix, I'd need many new parts. He offered to take the Mustang off my hands for $1500, but I couldn't do it. She and I have been together since 1965. She's been like my best friend. We'd been together too long and would stay together till death do us part.

Saturday night, I began packing. I hadn't heard from Ben, who usually dropped by, or at least called, every Saturday even if we didn't go out. It was just as well. All good things must come to an end. I'm not even sure it was a good thing. He wanted a wife and babies. Well, he'd had that and it didn't work out and I didn't want to end up writing out his child support checks for him each month while our kids went without. Not that I wanted kids. I mean, I like kids well enough, don't get me wrong, but with Ben, well, he'd want me to stay home and take care of them.

I threw a pair of jeans in my suitcase, which lay open across my bed.

As I packed, I was feeling down, and up, and down again. It was Saturday night and I had no place to go. It's not healthy for people to be home alone on Saturday night. At least that's my theory.

Not that Saturday nights had the same importance as fifteen or twenty years ago, but still I was getting into a real rut when the doorbell rang. I put my eye to the peephole. It was Ben, all six foot four inches of him. I wasn't sure if that was good or bad, but at least he'd fill the void in my evening.

I pulled open the door and cast my eyes down demurely.

"Why, Ben what a surprise."

"Hi, Mavis," his deep voice rumbled.

I closed the door behind him and we stood there staring at each other in a moment of silence. When my neck started getting a crick in it from looking up at him, I asked him to sit down.

"Want something to drink?"

"I want to talk."

"Can't talk and drink at the same time, huh?" I couldn't help myself, it just slipped out.

"Don't be flippant," he said harshly.

"Gee, I'm sorry. What do you want me to be?"

"I want you to be serious for once and talk to me." His face softened.

"Let's start over then. May I offer you something to drink? Coffee, tea, soft drink, beer, bourbon, scotch, vodka—"

"Damnit, there you go again."

"I can't help the way I am. I thought it was one of my most endearing characteristics. At least, that's what you used to say."

"All right. Get me a bourbon, but then I want to talk."

"Wait. Is this an official visit or a social call?"

His eyes became slits as he stood up. "I'm off duty."

"Oh. Okay. Bourbon it is." I turned to go toward my tiny kitchen, but he quickly grabbed my arm and pulled me to him. Boy, did he lay one on me. A kiss, I mean. When we came up for air, I was breathless. The fact that he leaves me that way is one of the reasons we still see each other. "What was that for?" I asked when I could speak again.

"On account of as how," he answered with a grin.

"What?"

"On account of as how I want you to know my feelings haven't changed."

"I was wondering."

"Can I get that drink now?"

My turn to grin. "Yeah. Come with me into the kitchen." He got a bourbon and water and I got a Lite, a fine pilsner beer. We traipsed back past my little dinette into the living room, where we sat next to each other on the couch. I was hoping for some heavy necking.

Ben had other ideas. "Mavis," he said in a too businesslike manner, "you're the talk of the locker room."

"Don't beat around the bush, Ben. Just come right out and tell me what's on your mind." I can't help it. Facetiousness just comes naturally to me.

He rolled his eyes and I knew what was coming.

"Can't you be serious for one minute?"

"You're going to tell me that lumpy Lon has been slandering my good name." I put my drink down on the table and reached for my cigarettes. I was about to light up, which I've noticed I do when I'm in an avoidance situation—I've been analyzing it, see—when I was rudely interrupted.

"Have you started smoking again?"

"Is that what Lon has been saying about me? You'd think he'd have better things to talk about."

"No. He was laughing about your stupid theory. When did you start back?"

"It's not stupid. I'm right. Lon's the one who's stupid. Two weeks ago. I'm surprised you didn't smell it on my clothes when we went out to dinner."

"I was too busy trying to talk some sense into you, but I can see it didn't work. If you want to kill yourself, it's none of my business"

"That's right. Either way, you can't stop me. I'll smoke if I want to and I'll work my theory. Lon can work his. The dumb jerk. I knew he wouldn't believe me. I banked on it."

"He's actually a good detective."

"He's an asshole."

Ben whistled. "He must have made quite an impression."

"No different from the last time."

"Come on, Mavis. Did you really think he'd buy that dumb theory? There's no basis for it."

"Sure there is. I tried to tell him. I really did. He just has his own ideas. Well, I've got news for you, and for all of HPD. You all can just laugh your guts out in the locker room while I solve this murder."

"Sure, baby."

My turn to narrow my eyes. "Don't give me that. Don't patronize me, Ben. I'm serious. This is my big chance and I'm not going to blow it."

He was scooting over closer to me on the couch. Somehow the conversation had gone awry. Ben wasn't interested any more. No more chewing of my ass. No more sour looks. I suddenly became confused. Why was he here? Just to tell me that all of Houston was laughing?

"What's going on?" I asked him as I put my hands upon his chest and held him back. He kept coming. "What is it? I'm not a threat anymore? Everything's okay because I'm not a menace to the insecurities of the men of the HPD?"

"Let's forget it for right now, Mavie. I don't want to fight. It's not worth it."

Now he was into heavy necking, but I was not. I was hurt. Was it so funny? I didn't mind lousy Lon and his buddies making fun behind my back, but if Ben agreed with them, well, that was different.

I was still trying to talk, but his face was too close to mine for eye contact. I'm big on eye contact. Then his face was buried beneath my hair, his mouth nibbling on my neck, his arms around me, pulling me closer. The importance of what I was trying to say was slipping away from me as I felt a tingling. Much as I was trying to resist, I couldn't help myself. When his lips came down on mine, I completely lost my train of thought.

A few minutes later we were headed past the kitchen to my bedroom, our clothing leaving a trail behind us. We had firm intentions of coming together upon my bed, but there was one little item that I'd forgotten about.

Ben pulled up short of the bed and abruptly stopped what he was doing. Dammit.

"Going somewhere?" His tone was as sharp and cold as an icicle.

My heart was palpitating for more reasons than one. My eyes followed his, and there, yawning open across the width of my double bed, the evidence of a trip in the making plain to see, was my suitcase.

I searched for a glib answer.

"I asked you a question."

The temperature had dropped from the high nineties to the freezing point in about five seconds flat. I saw no use in stalling or telling him anything other than the truth. My eyes roved over his face as we both stood staring from my suitcase to each other and back at my suitcase again.

I started toward the bed to close my luggage. "Oh, I'm driving over to Austin tomorrow to visit an old friend. We're going to spend the day together, and then I'll be coming back home Monday after she goes to work. She wanted me to come for the whole weekend, but it's been so hot that I didn't want to drive when my air-conditioner was broken, so today I got Alex, you know, Vivian's husband, to fix it for me. I could have left late this afternoon, but I didn't get packed because I didn't know how long it would take Alex to fix it and I thought I might as well wait and get up early tomorrow. I guess I could have flown, but I needed to get my air-conditioner fixed anyway, and you know how I hate to be without my car when I go anywhere. There." I had the suitcase all latched and placed on the floor and stood facing Ben, ready to resume where we'd left off.

He was staring down at me with that narrow-eyed look of his—the look I'm sure he reserves only for me and prisoners to whom he gives the third degree.

"What?" I asked.

"Where are you really going?"

I don't know why he didn't believe it. It sounded like a perfectly good story to me. "I told you. I'm going to Austin to visit a friend. We're going to have a picnic at Barton Springs and go swimming. She's been having some problems with her husband and she called me to talk about it. She's always called me when she has problems; she says that she's never found another friend she can confide in like she can me; and then she said she wanted me to come for the weekend. But I couldn't bear to drive in the heat, like I told you."

"I don't believe you," Ben said as he started back down the hall. He began picking up pieces of his clothing.

"Ben, why would I lie about a little thing like that?" I asked as I followed him. He was getting dressed.

"I don't know where you're going, but it's not Austin. I suspect that wherever it is, it's tied to that murder case."

"I'm going to Austin to visit a friend. She works in the Capitol Building. She's the secretary for one of the state representatives. If he's in town on Monday, she might even introduce me to him before I leave." By this time he was sitting on the couch tying his shoes. I watched while he buttoned up his shirt and slipped on his tan suit coat.

"Ben, why are you so angry?"

"I'm not going to argue with you, Mavis," he said and began knotting his tie. "I know you're lying and it makes me mad. I told you to leave the case alone, but you won't do it. I thought it was all a joke to you or that you were through with it, but I see you aren't."

"I'm going to Austin to see a friend; that's all, Ben. Why won't you believe me?" I was on the point of pleading as I stood there half naked. I could see that the warmth was oozing out of our relationship.

"Quit lying," he said as he approached the front door.

"How can you do this? How can you just get dressed and leave me like this?" My voice was getting shrill.

"When you're ready for an open, honest relationship, Mavis, call me. I might still be around." With that, Ben flung open the door and left, slamming it so hard behind him that the windows rattled.

I stood there gaping after him. It had all happened so fast that I was somewhat in shock. I tried to think of where I'd gone. wrong. It was a situation of damned if you do and damned if you don't. How could we have an open, honest relationship when he tried to tell me what to do? I turned the lock and began picking up my clothes. There was nothing to do except go to bed with the late movie. I'd think more about Ben tomorrow.

Chapter 13

ON SUNDAY, I DEPARTED FOR AUSTIN. I took Highway 290 west out of Houston and cruised into the hill country around six o'clock that night. It's not a bad drive. Boring, about four hours of highway bordered by beautiful blankets of bluebonnets, our state flower, but all in all, not a bad drive.

I called my friend while I was there, but she wasn't home. Sunday evening I bought a chicken dinner and went out to Barton Springs for a solitary picnic under the trees. I watched the kids swimming in the icy spring water, and the lovers making out on blankets on the far bank, and felt a little sorry for myself.

Monday morning I connived for three hours at the University of Texas till finding out that Doris Jones was really Elizabeth Anne Reynolds of Fort Worth. She had been a partner in the law firm of Spencer and Reynolds. Her home was in Arlington, Texas. She had been a member of the alumni association until last year. I took down her office and home addresses before I left.

After that, by a long-distance call to Carl, I okayed a trip to Fort Worth. Carl also informed me that a "great big cop" was looking for me. That would be Ben. I immediately felt better except that Carl told him that I really was in Austin.

Lastly, I made contact with a panicky Margaret. It seems that Mavis Davis Productions was finally in demand to produce. She'd had calls on several subpoenas, a background investigation, and a home study. After numerous monotonous minutes of encouragement, I convinced her that she was capable of doing the work all by her little self, told her my plans, and cut loose.

By Monday noon, this young woman—or so I keep telling myself—was headed north on Interstate 35. It would take approximately four hours to make my destination. Less if I ignored that ridiculous double-nickel law, which I could hardly resist doing. After all, there were some areas where it was legal to do sixty-five. Not that I drove as slowly as sixty-five.

The questions were spinning around and around in my brain, and the adrenaline was flowing again. My foot was like lead strapped to the accelerator as I left the true hill country behind and aimed for the soft slopes of northern Texas.

Chapter 14

AT A CONVENIENCE STORE ON THE outskirts of Arlington, I bought a street map of the Fort Worth-Dallas area. It had been years since my childhood visits to Six Flags Over Texas, an amusement park slightly smaller than Disneyland, way before Interstate 20—which runs from Fort Worth, through Arlington and some other bedroom communities, to Dallas—was finished. Even though I roughly knew my way around, I didn't want to waste precious time on wrong turns.

The second thing I did was say a prayer. Then I gathered up my nerve while I was still getting a rush and drove, almost straight, to the Reynolds' homestead.

Situated in a small, exclusive subdivision just a leap from the new interstate, the house was a split-level ranch style on about a half-acre lot immersed in maple trees and lots of other greenery. It would have fallen in the $100-to-200-thousand range by Houston standards. I was suitably impressed.

I parked across the street and surveyed the area for a moment. I and my poor little Mustang felt shabby and out of place. In that neighborhood we were like a solitary blemish on an otherwise clear complexion. With my luck, if I lurked too long, the neighbors would call the police.

Finally, I forced myself out of the car and approached the front door, my fingers crossed. If my luck held, the family would still live there. My palms became sweaty the minute my finger pushed the doorbell. I waited. My eyes swept the portals of the adjacent homes. No one made an appearance. Nor did anyone open the door in front of which I was standing. I rang again and waited. Nothing. Talk about frustration. I'd gotten all nervous over nothing.

Well, I had two choices. I could wait or I could go see her partner. I chose the latter. When I got back into the car, I looked up the office address in Fort Worth and headed west.

It was almost four-thirty when I reached the address of Spencer and Reynolds. Surprisingly, the building was in what I'd normally consider a lower-class, but-not-quite-sleazy, neighborhood in the older part of town. I'd been expecting something on par with the house I'd just left. The building at least predated the Korean War, and possibly World War II. The foyer's ceiling was more than twenty feet high and hanging down from it was an old crystal chandelier. The walls were paneled halfway up with what appeared to be mahogany. The floor was cracked marble.

The elevator wasn't working, so I climbed the dimly lit stairs to the fourth floor. There was very little activity anywhere. I was not at all at ease during my ascent. The building was in a bad state of disrepair and appeared to have very few tenants. When I finally found the suite of offices listed on the law school alumni form, they were vacant.

I searched up and down the hall until I found a talkative young lady who reminded me very much of Candy. She told me that the previous year the building had been purchased for renovation. All tenants were being forced to move. Did she know anything about Spencer and Reynolds? No, just my luck, she had been hired only recently.

My first inclination was to borrow a chair and sit down for a good cry. I was tired and thirsty. I hadn't stopped for lunch and my stomach was growling at five-minute intervals. I felt sticky and uncomfortable. But I wasn't defeated. I thanked her and descended the gloomy staircase.

Back out on the street in the declining north Texas sun, I spotted an antiquated drug store catty-comer from where I stood. I crossed over to it and went inside in search of a phone book. It appeared to be a mom-and-pop operation. Mom, who was behind the soda fountain, directed me to a real, genuine, wooden phone booth, like the kind Superman used. It was in the back of the store, hidden behind a magazine and card rack. Superman wouldn't have needed directions because of his X-ray vision.

I slipped inside and closed the door. The light came on, exposing unique inscriptions and wood carvings, probably left by the neighborhood youth corps, but the phone book was mostly intact. I sat down and flipped through it, letting my fingers do the you know what.

Spencer and Reynolds no longer existed, but Vernon Spencer, Attorney at Law, did. I copied down the address and replaced the book. Glancing at my watch, I didn't have much hope of catching him in the office, so decided to stop at the fountain for a Coke.

Mom was a short, elderly little lady with blued hair who appeared to be in her early seventies. She wore a full-length apron over her flowery, shirtwaist dress. I smiled at her as I put my briefcase on her counter and seated myself upon one of the stools that was permanently bolted down. I let my shoes fall off and clatter to the floor and put my stockinged feet up on the ledge.

"We're about to close," she said.

"Oh, I'm terribly sorry. I just … thought … nevermind." I reached for my briefcase in disappointment. I was really thirsty more than anything else, but it could wait.

"You look tired."

"Yeah. It's been a long trip," I said as my feet groped around for my shoes.

"Where you from?"

"Houston."

"Just get here?"

"A little while ago."

"Nonstop trip?"

"Yes. Well, I drove up from Austin this morning." I turned to leave.

"Well, sit down then. I'm not in that big a hurry. Just like to close around five or so, before dark, you know, 'cause it's not that safe around here then."

"Thanks. Sure you don't mind?"

"I wouldn't offer if I did. Sit down and make yourself comfortable. What can I get for you?"

"Just a Coke would be fine." I sat back down and let my shoes slip off again.

She chuckled. "You're hungry I'll bet."

I shrugged my shoulders. "I can wait."

"How about a nice club sandwich, a glass of milk, and a piece of my homemade apple pie. I still have a slice left."

I grinned at her when my stomach rumbled. "That would be great if it's not too much trouble."

"No bother. I'd just throw the pie out or take it home for my husband. I bake fresh pies every morning 'cause everybody around here loves 'em. You just sit there and relax, and I'll have it all up in a jiffy." She turned her back on me and went down the way a bit and began pulling out all the fixings from an old refrigerator at the end of the bar.

I took a moment to look around. It was as if I'd stepped back into the thirties. There was a room off to one side with a caged window and lettering that said PHARMACY. I could see a bald head bobbing around behind the packages of medications that were piled up on the shelves. I took it that Pop was the pharmacist.

The walls were lined with shelves of small gift items, perfume, and makeup. There were a few small wooden tables and chairs in the back near the phone booth. My eyes swept back to the counter that displayed real soda fountains and red-topped gallon jars of what used to be penny candy. I watched while Mom popped a cone-shaped paper cup into a metal holder and pulled a handle. She filled the cup with water and came back smiling as she placed it in front of me.

"That'll get you started," she said. "Nothing like a cold drink of water."

I gulped it down. She was right.

"Whatcha doing up here in our neck of the woods?" she called over her shoulder as she began putting the sandwich together after she pulled the toasted bread from a small toaster oven.

"Checking on somebody," I called back.

"You a police woman or something?"

I hesitated, then decided it couldn't hurt to tell her. "Sort of an investigator."

"Oh. Well, isn't that nice. You make your living that away?"

"I'm trying. I do a lot of stuff like serving subpoenas and doing home studies for adoptions and child custody cases. This is my first case like this one."

She came over and placed in front of me a large white plate piled high with a triple-decker sandwich and potato chips. "There," she said, pleased with herself. Then she pulled some napkins from a metal container and set them beside the plate, shuffled back to the refrigerator, poured me a tall glass of milk, and brought it back. "Eat up."

I took a huge bite and closed my eyes as I began chewing. I knew she was watching me, but I couldn't help it. It was just what I needed and I intended to enjoy it.

"So who're you looking for? Anybody I'd know?"

With my mouth full, I stared across at her and held up one finger. When I'd swallowed, I said, "This is great. Thanks so much. I'm not looking for anyone. Well, I am, but I've found him, or I will if the address in the phone book is accurate. I'm checking on someone though." I took another bite.

As I chewed, Mom pulled up a tall wooden stool and perched on it as she stared across the counter at me. "So who're you checking on? Or is it not proper to ask?"

Again I had to finish chewing. Then I took a gulp of milk that was so cold it made my teeth hurt. "Elizabeth Reynolds." I wasn't prepared for the look of shock that flashed across the old lady's face. I almost choked on the third bite. Her eyes got large and the skin tightened across her wrinkled face as she grimaced.

Chapter 15

"DID YOU KNOW HER?" I ASKED after a lot of rapid chewing and swallowing.

"Oh, yes. Everyone in the neighborhood knew Elizabeth, good and bad alike. She grew up here. She used to come in here when she was a little girl. Her parents lived just around the corner."

"Really? Are they still there? Can you give me their address?"

She shook her head slowly. "No. They passed on a few years before Elizabeth disappeared." Her eyes took on a faraway look. "She was an only child. Born late in their lives. She came as a big surprise." The old lady smiled then, a twinkle in her eye. "A good one though. They raised her with as much energy as if they were twenty years younger. She died. Elizabeth's mother, I mean. And six months later, he followed her. Elizabeth was heartbroken." She shook her head at me. "Elizabeth was like a daughter to all of us around here."

"Oh. That's too bad."

"Why? Do you know where Elizabeth is? Have you found her?"

I carefully avoided answering. "Tell me, Mrs...."

"Newbold."

"Mrs. Newbold." I held out my hand toward her. "My name is Mavis Davis." We shook. Her hand was soft and frail, but she took mine firmly. "Did you know her partner? And her family?" "Oh, yes. I didn't like him much. The partner, I mean. Vernon Spencer." She practically spit out his name. "She met him in Austin at law school. She talked him into coming back here and going in with her. She'd always sworn that she was going to come back to the old neighborhood and set up practice when she got out of school. I didn't believe her, but she did. Right across the street in the old Barham building."

"Yeah, I know. I was there before I came here, but the office isn't there anymore."

"Spencer moved practically right after Elizabeth left. He couldn't wait to get out of here. He didn't belong. He was after big money, he was, but not content to wait for it to come to him. You know the type I mean."

"Yes."

"Well, I never liked him. He didn't have the time of day for us from the very beginning. He wouldn't even come in here for lunch like Elizabeth did. Always took his downtown or someplace fancy somewhere. Like him. Fancy-pants sort of person with big ideas."

"What about her husband? Did you know him?"

"Sure, and the kids, too—two of the most beautiful girls you ever saw. He's a local boy. They were high school sweethearts. They got married right after graduation and Elizabeth put him through school and had the babies while he got his education. He's a professor at the university in Arlington."

"What's he like?"

"He's an all right sort, I guess. Nothing special to my mind." I had the impression that no one would be good enough for Elizabeth as far as Mrs. Newbold was concerned, but I didn't say so. I took another bite of my sandwich while I thought about what she'd told me. Hearing footsteps behind me, I turned around and saw an old man approaching the counter area.

"Newey, this is Miss Davis. She's been asking about Elizabeth Reynolds," Mrs. Newbold said by way of introduction. "This is my other half, Miss Davis."

I smiled, and swallowed, and held out my hand toward the old man. He was not much taller than she was. He was dressed in a white shirt and navy slacks and peered at me through a pair of bifocals. He shook my hand.

"Nice to meet you," I said.

"What about Elizabeth?" He eyed me suspiciously, his brow wrinkled. "You know her?"

"Not exactly. I'm checking on her background."

He perched on a barstool a couple down from me and crossed his arms in front of his chest. "For what? Why're you asking about her?"

I glanced from Pop to Mom. Her face had grown serious, and she was studying me. I knew if I was to get any more information out of them, I was going to have to show my hand. I inhaled deeply and let out a long sigh. They seemed like nice people who were concerned that my presence might not be in Elizabeth's best interest. I didn't know what to say except to come right out with it. I tried to be as gentle as possible, but how do you break news such as murder gently? I guess I'll never figure that one out. I looked back at Mr. Newbold. "I don't know how to tell you, but I've been hired by someone in Houston to look into Elizabeth's death."

Mrs. Newbold gasped and clutched her chest. And Mr. Newbold quickly trotted around the length of the counter and held her to him. She wrapped her arms around him and buried her face in his shirt. He stood there, eyes closed, letting out sharp breaths of air. God, I hated that.

I sat there, watching them, bowing my head, and then watching them again. I'd lost my appetite and pushed the plate away. I swallowed the remainder of the milk. I lit a cigarette and got up to look for an ashtray. I wandered around the store while they clung to each other. Finally, I brought the ashtray back from one of the tables and sat back down, waiting for one of them to speak.

"You gonna be all right, Mama?" he asked her as he pulled back and looked into her face.

She nodded and reached for a paper napkin. She wiped her face. "Let's close up."

Neither of them would look at me.

He let go of her and went to the front door. He pulled the shade down and turned the dead bolt with his key.

She got up from the stool and pushed it off to the side. Then she looked at me. "You finished?"

I nodded. "Yes."

"I'll rinse these things out. Then you'll come upstairs with us and tell us all about it."

"Yes." I felt like the grim reaper.

The three of us went up the stairs at the back of the store. Their home was a two-bedroom apartment. They took me into the living area and sat me down in an old armchair covered with a handmade afghan.

I told them what I knew and showed them the pictures. Mrs. Newbold wept some more. Mr. Newbold cleared his throat a lot. When I was through, Mrs. Newbold went into the kitchen and made a pot of coffee for them, tea for me, and returned with a tray full of fruit and sandwiches.

"I think you're right, Miss Davis," Mrs. Newbold said when she was situated on the sofa next to her husband. "It wasn't any serial killer."

"Please call me Mavis."

"Mavis," she said. "I think Vernon Spencer did it."

"Now, Mama, you don't know that." Mr. Newbold patted her hand gently.

"No, but I think he's the sort that's capable of it."

"Tell me, Mrs. Newbold. How long had Elizabeth been associated with Vernon Spencer?"

"A couple of years. Like I told you, she met him in law school. After Robert—that's her husband—finished school, it was her turn. She had only gone part-time before. Then Robert got a job teaching while she went to undergraduate school at the University of Texas at Arlington. They lived around here then. After she got through, they moved down to Austin for her to go to law school. He taught there. Then, when she was through, they moved back here. Well, not here, but to Arlington where he got another position. They bought a beautiful home out there."

"Yes, I know. I went there today."

"Then you've met Robert," Mr. Newbold said.

"No. No one was home, so I came over here."

"Oh my goodness! Robert and the girls don't know then," Mrs. Newbold said.

"Not to my knowledge." I shook my head at them. I hated to tell the husband and kids. I didn't know if I could take it.

"Oh my," she said again. "When are you going to tell them?"

"I don't know. I was tonight, but I'm awfully tired. I was thinking of calling and making an appointment with him for tomorrow evening. That way I'll be sure to catch him."

"That's a good idea. You don't want to tell him over the phone," Mr. Newbold said.

"No." I had several reasons for not wanting to do that, including the ever-present possibility that the husband did it, but I didn't say so.

"You can use our phone if you like. It's not long distance from here," Mrs. Newbold offered.

"Thank you. I will before I leave. What else can you tell me about Vernon Spencer?"

"Well," said Mrs. Newbold with a look at her husband, "like I told you, I never cared for the boy. He seemed too money hungry and impatient. He never did anything to us or anything, but he never did anything for somebody for which he didn't charge an arm-and-a-leg, you know?"

I nodded, trying to be patient.

"He was a young fella," Mr. Newbold said. "Quite a few years younger than Elizabeth. He wasn't married, and he didn't have any kids. He might be approaching thirty by now; I'm not sure."

"I don't think so, dear. He couldn't be a day over twenty-eight, I'd say."

"Maybe you're right. It doesn't matter. I do remember that he drove a fancy car and dressed good, right off. And from what Elizabeth said, he didn't come from money. She'd taken a liking to him and thought he'd fit in with us here. She wanted to help the people in the neighborhood, not that she didn't want to make money too, don't get me wrong. She earned a good living. But she worked hard, long hours making it."

"Spencer did the criminal part, Mavis. Elizabeth did some, but she liked to do wills, and she worked with the neighborhood kids, the ones that got into trouble. She also did divorce cases."

"And remember she represented Hagar when she got injured falling down those stairs when old-man Johnson wouldn't fix the apartment building," Mrs. Newbold said to her husband.

"Yes. That was the kind of thing she liked. Spencer, well, he was the lawyer for some really bad ones. A lot of them didn't even come from around here. We'd see them going in and out of the building across the street. We asked Elizabeth once."

"Spencer drank a lot, too, Mavis," Mrs. Newbold said. "I wouldn't be surprised if he wasn't drunk every night when he left the office. He kept a bottle up there."

"You don't know that, Mama," Mr. Newbold frowned at his wife.

"I do so. The cleaning lady told me. She'd put the empties out."

Mr. Newbold shrugged. "I don't know anything about that." I'd been watching them, my head turning from left to right, like watching a tennis match, as they carried on their conversation. And my appetite returned. I devoured half a sandwich and a couple of plums while all this was going on.

"And Robert, did she get along with him?" I asked.

"Far as we know, she did. We didn't see him hardly at all. He did drop by each Christmas with Elizabeth, to bring us a little gift," Mrs. Newbold said, her eyes misting over.

"And they brought the girls each year, too. So we could see how they'd grown and we'd give them each a little something." "They seemed to get along fine."

"Do you know if Elizabeth had any enemies? What do you think could have made her run off like that?" I asked.

They exchanged looks, and I couldn't tell if that meant anything or not. Then Mrs. Newbold shook her head.

"I can't think of a single person who would want to harm a hair on her head," Mr. Newbold said. "Even the people she went up against never threatened her or anything so far as I know. Seems like I would have heard about it."

Mrs. Newbold nodded. "Everyone loved her." Remembering Catherine's letter, I asked, "Do you know somebody named Madge?"

"Oh, yes," Mrs. Newbold chuckled. "Madge Hennesey. That would be Elizabeth's best friend. She's a funny girl. Came in with Elizabeth for lunch several times."

"Would you know how I could get in touch with her?"

Mr. Newbold shook his head.

Mrs. Newbold said, "She works at a bank. Can't remember which one, though. You'd have to ask Robert. He'd know."

I sighed. It was time to go. "Mind if I use your phone now?"

"No. You need the number?" Mrs. Newbold asked as she got up from the sofa and led me to the telephone in the kitchen. "Yes, please, do you have a phone book?"

"Better than that, I have the number up here on the wall. I've never marked it out. Every once in a while I call the girls just to see how they're doing." She smiled, and the smile wrinkles were like big clefts in her cheeks.

I called the Reynolds house. One of the girls answered. When I got Mr. Reynolds on the phone, I did no more than introduce myself and tell him that I was an investigator and needed to talk with him the following day about his wife.

His voice was deep, and he said in a resigned tone, "I thought that was all over."

"No, sir," I said. "It's being reopened and I'd like to speak with you in person, if I may."

He invited me out for four-thirty the following day. I thanked him, hung up, and shrugged at Mrs. Newbold.

"It isn't going to be easy," she said.

"I know, but I have to do it."

"It's the girls that I'm worried about."

"Yes. Well, I need to go now. I need to find a place to park myself before it gets real late." I smiled at her and slipped my arm across her shoulders. "You've been a big help."

"I hope so." Her voice sounded a little throaty.

We walked back through the dining room into the living area where we found Mr. Newbold looking out the blinds at the front window. He turned when he heard us.

"I'll walk you out, Mavis," he said. "It's not safe for you by yourself."

"Thanks, I appreciate that." I gave Mrs. Newbold a little hug and picked up my purse and briefcase. Mr. Newbold and I went back down the stairs where he flipped on one light so we could see our way to the front of the store. He unlocked the door and came out onto the sidewalk with me.

"I'll watch you until you get to your car. Is it that Mustang over there?"

"Yes, how'd you know?"

"Unfamiliar car in my neighborhood."

I laughed. "Maybe you should have been an investigator." He smiled. "Maybe so." He held out his hand and took mine and gave it a squeeze. "Be careful."

I nodded. "Why do you stay here?"

"It's our home."

I nodded again and started across the street.

He hollered after me. "Mavis, call us if there is anything at all that we can do."

Chapter 16

AFTER I GOT SETTLED IN MY motel room, I found myself restless and unable to sleep. The conversation with the Newbolds went round and round in my head. As tired as I was, I was anxious to proceed with the investigation.

To think that I already had a suspect in Vernon Spencer was almost too much for me to handle. I wondered if Mrs. Newbold was just bitter or if Spencer was really the type of person she described. I lay in bed turning things this way and that until finally I must have drifted off.

When I awoke the next morning, it was after nine. I'd forgotten to leave a wake-up call. I could have lashed myself with a wet noodle. I had planned to get an early start, to catch Spencer first thing.

I hurriedly donned the same skirt and blouse that I'd worn the previous day. If I was going to stay long, I'd have to get some more clothes soon since I hadn't packed for this long of a trip.

Spencer's office was located in a house about a mile north of downtown. I passed a grain elevator and a tough-looking industrial area before I found it. It was a two-story, white frame building with huge stained-glass windows. The landscaping alone would have to cost more than I earned in a year. The shrubs were sculptured into shapes of animals. Flowers blossomed on both sides of the walk. A large tree cast shade over the front of the building. I went up the steps to the front door, which was half wood and half stained glass, and next to it was an engraved sign about three foot square that read, *VERNON J. SPENCER, ATTORNEY AND COUNSELOR AT LAW.*

As I entered, I was not surprised to have to walk across carpeting at least a foot deep in order to reach a receptionist who looked like she just stepped out of the pages of Vogue. She was a young girl of about twenty or so. Her blond hair was perfect, her nails a $50 job, and her clothes, well, let's just say that I'd give my eye teeth to exchange mine for hers. When I asked for Mr. Spencer, she smiled at me, flashing teeth that would do a toothpaste ad justice, and announced that he was at the courthouse in trial. When I started asking more questions, she got up from her station and left the room saying I'd have to talk to Mr. Spencer's legal assistant.

The waiting room was decorated with huge potted plants, gold-framed posters of festivals and art shows, and thick-velvet sofas. The receptionist's desk was some kind of dark wood, cherry or mahogony, and was clear of clutter except for a designer telephone set. When I grew up, that was the kind of office I wanted to have. Except for velvet sofas. I'm not real keen on velvet.

My observations were disturbed by the appearance of another blonde. She was a carbon copy of the first one, or rather, the first was a carbon copy of this one, who was a few years older.

She looked me up, down, and sideways as she approached me, making me feel that I'd come from the wrong side of the tracks, then held out her hand and said, in a melodious tone, "Hello, I'm Miss Sanders, Mr. Spencer's legal assistant. What may I do for you today?"

I took her hand, but almost dropped it when we shook. Her skin was cold and clammy. Her shake was limp. Like a dead fish. "I'm Mavis Davis. I'm from Houston, up here investigating a case. I really need to talk with Mr. Spencer, but I understand he's in trial. Do you know when he'll be available?"

"No, I really don't, Miss Davis. We've been hoping for days that he'd return. We miss him so. But it's been simply weeks and the case hasn't even gone to the jury yet. I'm sorry. I just don't know what to tell you."

"Oh." I tried to hide my disappointment. "Well, maybe you can help me. Would you mind answering a few questions?"

"Well, I don't know. If it has anything to do with one of our clients, I'm afraid that would be confidential, and I'd have to get Mr. Spencer's permission." Her icy blue eyes stared at me without wavering.

"It's not about a client. It's about Elizabeth Reynolds."

Her eyes flickered just for an instant, cut over toward her duplicate; then she recovered herself. "Who?"

"Mr. Spencer's former law partner. Hey, how long have you been with him anyway?"

"One year this month. I'm the senior assistant. I was hired when he purchased this building, and I helped decorate it." She straightened up a bit, as if in an attempt to look down her nose at me, but I was taller, so my nose was higher than hers.

"I guess you didn't know Miss Reynolds then, did you?"

"It's fair to say that I've heard her name mentioned, but no, I didn't know her. You'd really have to see him, and I'm afraid that's impossible today."

"Well, what court's he in?"

"State district court, downtown."

"I guess I could go there then, couldn't I? Well, thanks so much for your help. You've been a doll." Truer words I've never spoken, for she did look artificial. I turned to leave.

"You can't see him there," she said, her tone as cold as death. "He's in trial and can't be disturbed."

"Thanks again," I said, flashing a grin over my shoulder as I headed for the door.

She called after me. "Really, you won't get to talk to him. You're wasting your time."

I nodded at her as I left.

Once downtown, I had to park several blocks away from the courthouse because there was a lot of construction going on. The courthouse was a beautiful old stone building that obviously used to be in the center of the town square, but now there were buildings that had been added right up next to it, and walkways were being constructed.

The brown building next door looked something like a church. The painted facade featured a lady or an angel in a robe. She was carved from white stone. She must have been forty feet tall, from the tip of what looked like wings raised over her head to the bottom of a block on which she appeared to be standing. She was all in white, with her hands folded crosswise on her chest, and a set of scales hanging from her hips. I wondered if she was supposed to symbolize justice or mercy.

The old building I had to go into had a tall set of granite stairs leading up to the wood and glass doors, and lots of high windows.

Since I serve papers in Houston, I know the district clerk's office is kind of like a control center for the courts. If I was lucky, I'd be able to find someone there to tell me in what courtroom Spencer was trying his case. I found the building directory on one of the marble walls, but to my surprise, I was in the wrong building. The appellate courts, the probate clerk, some county courts, and the county clerk were housed in that building. I shouldn't have been surprised. The Houston courts are divided up into many separate buildings, but for some reason I was expecting the Fort Worth court system to be contained all in one place. Asking directions, I found I had to go next door to find the district clerk's office.

In the next building. I found the district clerk's office, which looked much like those in Houston, cluttered, but a pretty blond girl—Why did everyone seem to be blond?—directed me across the street for criminal stuff. This was getting boring. It was hot and my head was swimming as I crossed through the construction zone to the third building.

This building was a real museum piece. Outside, it had a state historical marker that gave a brief rundown of Fort Worth's history. Mostly it housed adult probation and the district attorney's office. I finally found a clerk and, armed with a copy of the monthly docket sheet I eventually discovered the courtroom where Spencer's case was docketed. Don't ask me what building that was, I lost count, but think it was the fourth or fifth.

When I got off the elevator, I found a number of people hanging out in the hall. Each wore a badge that said *JUROR*. I walked over to the courtroom and peeked in the window set in one of the doors at the rear of the court. The docket sheet listed a case number, the name of the defendant, the charge—in this case delivery of a controlled substance—the prosecutor, Doyle Proctor, and the defense attorney, Vernon Spencer.

I could see two men up at the bench conferring with the judge who sat in a large armchair that was centered in some sort of arch that made it appear as if the room was a temple rather than a courtroom. But for the flags bordering each side of the temple, I would have thought I was in the wrong place. The computer at the clerk's end, the witness stand, and the jury box also clued me in.

One of the men was white, with light-brown hair and a sculptured profile like that of a Greek God. He wore a sleek-fitting suit and highly polished shoes. He was gesturing madly with his hands, as if trying to make a point.

The other man was young-looking and black. His hair was closely cropped, his skin more yellow than brown, and his dark brown eyes were flashing as he made what looked like a rebuttal argument to the judge. He wore a light-brown tailored suit, spit-polished brown loafers, and his tie dangled loosely from his neck as he did a lot of gesturing.

The judge was relaxed in his chair, rocking back and forth as he listened to and watched the men. I shifted my position a little and could see another man sitting at one of the tables. He was watching the first two. A few spectators were in the audience, whispering to each other.

I looked back at the bench. Judging from the secretaries back at his office, the Greek God must be Vernon Spencer. He was a looker all right. I could picture him in that office, giving orders, being worshipped by the clones he hired. It was understandable why Mrs. Newbold might not take a liking to him. It was unlikely that he'd be happy in her neighborhood.

I got directions to the judge's office. When I entered, I was met by a jolly-looking, roly-poly lady of about fifty or so. Her little, light-blue eyes peered out at me through granny glasses. Her expression was friendly as she invited me in and asked me to close the door.

"I'm Mavis Davis," I said after making sure the door caught behind me.

"Georgia Eden," she said. "What can I help you with?"

"I'm looking into a case in Houston, and I need to talk with Vernon Spencer. Could you tell me when the judge might take a break?"

"Honey, you just missed it. He won't break again until lunch."

"Oh." If it wasn't for bad luck …

"You can set your clock by Judge Henry's breaks. Ten-thirty ever' mornin' and three o'clock ever' afternoon. Sorry 'bout that. He breaks for lunch at noon if you want to wait."

I glanced at my watch. Noon wasn't for another hour and fifteen minutes. "No, I don't think so. Guess I'll try to get some other things done and come back."

"You can leave Vern a note and I'll just add it to his pile," she said, indicating a stack of pink slips.

"You don't mind?"

"Nah. Here," she pushed her message book and a pen across her desk at me. "Write it out and I'll be sure to see that he gets it."

I leaned over her desk and wrote a brief note to Vernon Spencer, asking him to call me at my motel. Then I handed the book back to her.

"I wonder if you'd mind telling me something," I said to her.

"If I know it," she said.

"You know Vernon Spencer very well?"

She shrugged. "As well as any of the other lawyers that practice in our court."

"What kind of cases does he do mostly?"

"Criminal. Drug cases, murder, that kind of thing."

"Ugh."

"Yeah, but someone has to do them."

"Is Mr. Spencer well liked?"

"He's all right, I guess. Of course, I have my favorites like anyone, but he's okay."

"Would you describe him as ambitious?"

"Very," she said, and then laughed. "But then what lawyer isn't? Take Doyle out there. He's planning on being the next district attorney."

"The black attorney? That'll be a first, won't it?"

"Oh, honey, you don't know Vernon Spencer? He's the black attorney. Doyle is the white one."

"Boy! Am I confused. For some reason I thought the reverse was true."

"Do they have a lot of black prosecutors in Houston?"

"Yes. They come and go like all the rest."

"Well, that's why, I guess. You don't get many up here, but the numbers are improving all the time." She smiled at me. "And women, too."

"Well, that's good."

"Yes. As soon as they realize they're being treated like anyone else, it will be."

I nodded. I was anxious to leave. "Well, Georgia, it was nice meeting you. Hope I see you again sometime."

"You come by anytime."

"Thanks a lot for your help."

"You're welcome. I'll be sure to see that he gets your message."

"Thanks again." I left the office, being careful to close the door again behind me. Glancing into the courtroom on my way out, I could see that the jury was back in its box, and now Vernon Spencer was sitting at the table with the man who had been there alone before. Doyle Proctor was positioned at the table that was the closest to the jurors.

I mentally berated myself for making assumptions about people. When I thought about Mrs. Newbold's statements though, it made sense that Spencer was black. It would be understandable for Elizabeth Reynolds to bring him back to her old neighborhood, to persuade him to work with the inner city youth and the poor.

I left the courthouse and walked a few blocks until I got to the offices of the Fort Worth Star Telegram. After making a reasonable explanation to them, I got in to see their old copies.

For the remainder of the day, I checked the headlines and the police columns of each issue. There were rapes, robberies, muggings, burglaries, assaults, child-abuse cases, drug cases. There was a large drug bust eighteen months ago. Then I came to an issue that reported that Elizabeth Reynolds, a local attorney, was missing. Foul play was suspected, but there was no evidence to back up the police supposition. There were articles wherein her family was mentioned. An interview with Vernon Spencer was in a Sunday issue. Her disappearance was mentioned in less prominence throughout the papers as time went by. Then, nothing.

I continued to scan the papers until I got to the present date. Elizabeth was forgotten. Life went on.

Chapter 17

IT WAS MIDAFTERNOON WHEN I STEPPED back onto the streets of downtown Fort Worth. The sun bore down so intensely on the pavement that in my thin-soled flats, I felt as if I was walking on hot coals. The glare and the heat were as bad as Houston, except it wasn't as humid.

Once again I had missed lunch. Stopping a passerby, I received directions to the Tandy Center, a shopping mall that went underground. There was an ice-skating rink, a Radio Shack, a subway train—but not like New York's, more like the people movers at Disneyworld—and lots of small shops. I took the escalator down to a place called Japanese Beef or Chicken Bowl, where I got a huge plate of chow mein, an egg roll, and some iced tea. It was three-thirty by the time I swallowed the last bite.

I drove back to Arlington, parked my car across from the Reynolds house again, and waited. The birds were twittering in the trees. One flew after-and-was-pecking at a squirrel skittering across the road.

After a few minutes, a school bus arrived, moving slowly through the streets of the subdivision, stopping at every other corner to let out children. It proceeded past me as I waited in my parked car, then eased to a stop not far from the Reynolds' house. Three children got off. The two boys ran past me. The girl walked slowly to the mailbox, retrieved the mail, and, glancing through it, walked the rest of the way up the concrete path to the front door. She unlocked the door and went in, closing it behind her. That would be Anne.

Shortly thereafter, a recent-model Japanese compact car, its tires spinning, raced into the driveway and stopped. An older girl got out and went inside. That would be Catherine. A real beauty. Classic looks.

I continued to wait. Given the time of day and the tree under which I'd parked, the heat was not so bad. Four-thirty came and with it was Mr. Reynolds, right on the dot. He was driving a rundown, dust-covered Ford sedan. He got out, spotted me, and immediately waved me over. I knew my car stuck out like a sore thumb.

I jogged over to him, held out my hand, and breathlessly announced myself. I was going to have to get some more exercise. His handshake was firm. A good sign.

"What can I do for you, Miss Davis?" he asked. "Like I said yesterday, I thought I was through discussing my wife's disappearance." His tone was almost rude, but I suppose I couldn't blame him. I watched his face. He had kind-looking features, smile wrinkles around his mouth and eyes, but he looked tired. His hair was gray at the temples where in the photograph it had been a dark blond. He was about my height, and we looked each other straight in the eye.

I suddenly felt awkward and out of place. "Could we please go inside somewhere private and talk?"

"Whatever it is that you want, you can ask me out here. I'm not going to put the kids through any more questioning."

"Mr. Reynolds, I don't want to question your kids. I have some news about your wife and I thought you'd want to hear it in the privacy of your home rather than on the street."

"What kind of news?" His eyebrows drew together; his head cocked to one side.

I sighed. "Not good."

"I'm sorry?"

"Bad news, sir." I reached into my purse and pulled out the family portrait. "That is, if this was your wife."

"Where did you get this photograph?" he asked, snatching it out of my hand. He stared at it, and then, looking back at me, said, "What do you mean if this was my wife?"

I felt about two feet high. I hadn't expected him to be so defensive. I'd thought we'd be sitting down in the den or someplace and I'd break it to him gently. Now I didn't know what to do. I shrugged my shoulders and gestured helplessly at him, not sure what to say. "If you'd just let me sit down and explain it to you," I said hesitantly.

"Are you saying she's dead?" His voice was loud, demanding, angry.

"Please, Mr. Reynolds, calm down a minute." I took him by the arm and guided him toward the door. "Let's go inside." I opened the door and Catherine came up to me.

"What's going on?" she asked.

"Hi. I'm Mavis Davis. I'm here to discuss some business with your father. It's okay. Is there somewhere I can talk to him in private?"

"The den," she said, pointing to it.

"Please, Mr. Reynolds, let's go into the den, okay?"

"It's all right, Catherine," Mr. Reynolds said, having sufficiently recovered himself. "Miss Davis and I just have some things to discuss. Go on."

"Okay, Dad. Nice to meet you, Miss Davis."

I nodded at her, and Mr. Reynolds and I walked into the den.

He sat down on the edge of a recliner very similar to the one in Doris Jones's apartment. I closed the door and dragged an ottoman over in front of him and sat down.

"Where did you get this picture?" he repeated.

"At the apartment of a woman named Doris Jones, in Houston."

He shook his head. "I don't know anyone by that name."

I shook my head back at him. My heart was pounding, and I felt queasy in my stomach. "I don't expect you to recognize her name, Mr. Reynolds, but I believe that Doris Jones was your wife, Elizabeth Reynolds." I pulled out the other photograph, the one Carl had given me.

He took it and compared it with the first. "She's dead?" he asked softly. His dark-blue eyes were watery.

"Yes."

"Why do you think she was my wife?"

"The man she was working for identified her from that picture. We also found some jewelry in a safe deposit box in Doris' name." I pulled out the rings from the side pocket of my purse and handed them to him.

Looking down at the rings, he uttered, "Oh, God!" His hand wrapped around the jewelry tightly. His eyes squeezed shut, and his whole face wrinkled up as though he'd just been fatally wounded.

"I'm sorry," I said, and put my hand on his. I felt the tears stinging my eyes.

A few minutes later, he got up. "I want to talk to you, Miss Davis, but not now. Could you come back later?"

"Sure." I pulled out a card and wrote the name of the motel in which I was staying on the back of it. "Call me when you want to talk," I said, handing him the card.

He slipped the card in the pocket of his suit coat and nodded. His face looked gray. His eyes were wide and staring.

"Are you going to be okay?" I asked.

"Yes. I'd just like to be alone with the girls."

"I understand." I left him there like that, standing, staring, a dazed expression on his face. I let myself out of the den, then out of the house. I went back to my car and back to Fort Worth.

After stopping at a department store and buying some hose, underclothes, and a summer suit off the sale rack, I went to my motel for a shower and a change.

When I got out of the shower, I called Margaret at home. "You didn't call me last night," she complained.

"I'm sorry, Margaret. I got distracted and didn't get a room until dark. What's going on?"

"You'll never guess. I dyed my hair back."

"Marvelous. What made you do that?"

"Bernie."

"Bernie?"

"Yeah, my new boyfriend. You wouldn't believe what he said I looked like with blond hair."

I could well imagine. "I didn't know you had a boyfriend, Margaret. That's great."

"Yeah. I met him at the courthouse. He works in the district clerk's office. He would talk to me every time I went there to pick up some papers for one of our clients. Finally we went out to lunch. Then to a movie one night. Well, you know how it goes, Mavis. Now things are really warming up!"

"That's really neat, Margaret. I'm glad for you. Has Ben called?"

"No."

"Oh." I tried to keep the disappointment out of my voice. "You know he never calls you much at the office, Mavis."

"It doesn't matter. How's Candy?"

"She's fine. She was hoping you'd call today and tell us what's going on. You know how hyper she gets."

"Well, you can tell her everything's going fine. I met some people yesterday that knew Elizabeth Reynolds ever since she was little. That's why I didn't call yesterday evening. I stayed and talked to them for a long time. Then I found a room and, well, by the time I got around to it, it was so late."

"Did you go to her office? Did you tell her family?" Her excited voice squeaked in my ear.

"Calm down. Yes, on both counts. But her office isn't an office anymore. Her partner moved into this ritzy, old house near downtown. You should see it. It looks like he's into some big money. And Margaret, guess what."

"What?"

"He's black, and he's got these two gorgeous blond, white secretaries. You wouldn't believe how beautiful they are."

"Really? Did you get to talk to him?"

"No. He's in trial. I left this number and I'm hoping he'll call tonight. I did talk to her husband though. You ought to see their house. It's out in this woodsy area of Arlington, a real expensive section almost like River Oaks or something."

"Wow. They must have money. What's he like?"

"I'm not really sure. He had a friendly type of face, but I haven't had much of a chance to get to know him yet. He got upset when I broke the news."

"Was it real sad?"

"Yes and no. I don't know what I expected. I guess men don't get hysterical like women. He was upset, but then he asked me to leave. He's supposed to call me later, too."

"Doesn't sound like you're accomplishing much, Mavis. I mean for two whole days up there."

"I am and I'm not. I kind of feel like I'm treading water in a way. I've been giving out information and not receiving any except for those people yesterday. They're convinced the partner did it."

"Why?"

"I'm not sure. They said he's money hungry, and they don't like him. I'm going to have to think about it a lot. Hopefully tomorrow I'll get to spend some time with the partner, Spencer, and the family. I'll keep you posted."

"Okay. Hey, Mavis, want me to keep on with the study?"

"What?" I remembered the case Margaret was working on. "Oh, yeah. Is it going okay?"

"Yes."

We talked about what she was doing for a little while, and then hung up.

I dressed and went to dinner in the motel. It felt great to have some clean clothes and sit down to a proper meal. When I got back to my room, it was approaching nine and I was just getting ready to call Carl when the phone rang.

"Mavis Davis?" a muffled voice asked.

"Yes."

"Go home."

I was startled. I couldn't tell if it was a man's voice or a woman's—it was so whispery. "What did you say?"

"Butt out of the Reynolds thing or you'll be sorry," the voice breathed.

A shiver ran up my spine. "Who is this?" I demanded with much more courage than I felt.

The phone clicked in my ear. Then there was a dial tone.

Chapter 18

B **EING THE DEVOUT COWARD THAT I** am, when I hung up
the phone I was shaking in my shoes. I immediately dialed Carl's
number. I needed to hear the reassuring tones of someone from
home. I should have called the police, but since I was messing in police
business, the little voice inside my head told me that they wouldn't be too
awfully sympathetic.

With a falsely cheerful lilt in my voice, I inquired as to Carl's well-being.

"What's the matter, Mavis? You sound strange," Carl said.

"I think I'm making progress, Carl. Don't be alarmed, but I just got
off the phone with some creep that urged me to go home." I tried to keep
my voice from shaking. In fact, I tried to resist the urge to break down. I
couldn't let it get to me if I was going to be a successful detective, could I?

"Who was it?"

"I don't know. Unfortunately, whoever it was didn't see fit to
identify himself."

"Was it a man or a woman? What did they say? Did they threaten you?
Are you okay?"

"Whoever it was undoubtedly was full of hot air. The voice was strange, like he or she was talking through a hand or covered the phone or something. Anyway, not to worry." What's not to worry? But I had to put on a brave front. "So like I said, Carl, I must be making progress. Right?"

"Mavis, who knows where you're staying? Who would know to call you there?" Carl, I must say, was sounding rather worried. It was comforting. If only he wasn't a couple of hundred miles away.

"I left my name and the motel name with Mr. Reynolds and with a secretary at the courthouse where Vernon Spencer, Elizabeth's former law partner, was trying a case. It won't do any good to speculate, Carl, because Spencer or the secretary could have let anyone see that note. I have no way of knowing who knows me or what I'm doing here."

"Mavis, you've got to be careful. Don't make light of this. Is your door locked? You gotta gun?"

"Yes, the door's locked. And no, I don't believe in guns. They're just for killing people and I don't intend to kill anyone. I'll be okay. Is there any more news there? Has lumbering Lon been hassling you? Have the police turned up anything else that might tell who did it?"

"I think he misses you, Mavis." Carl laughed. "He came in today wanting to know why you haven't been around."

"Who did? Lon?"

"Yeah. He wanted to know if I bought that story line you'd given him."

"What did you tell him?"

"That I'd hired you, and that I thought you were good, and if he had any sense he'd have listened to you."

"You didn't!"

"Yeah, I did. He didn't like it too much, and huffed and puffed a lot, but he finally left. They're probably having a pow wow about you right now downtown."

"Oh, great. Next they'll be coming up here after me."

"Maybe that's not such a bad idea."

"Anyone but Lon, and it wouldn't be."

"Well, I could tell your boyfriend where you are."

"Don't you dare. That's not even funny. He's pretty angry as it is."

"Worried's more like it. He was here today, too."

It may be mushy, but when he said that, my heart leapt. Ben hadn't given up on me after all. "What did he say, Carl?"

"Wanted to know where you were and when you were coming back. I told him that when I heard from you I'd ask you to call him. Hey, Mavis, I think he's serious about you. Why don't you give him a chance? Seems like a nice enough guy."

I had to smile at Carl's words. My love life was getting to be more of a topic of conversation than his case. "I appreciate your thoughts on the matter, and I'll keep them in mind. Just continue stalling him for me, will you? And Lon, too." I gave him the name of the motel and my room number before hanging up, and extracted a promise that he'd keep the information to himself.

Just touching base with someone from home made me feel better. I undressed, turned on the TV, and got under the covers. Even if anyone called, I didn't hear the phone. It wasn't long after my head hit the pillow that I fell asleep.

The following day I received a phone call before I'd even gotten out of bed. It was Mr. Reynolds. He apologized for his behavior of the night before and asked me to come over that afternoon. I agreed.

I didn't know what to do with myself until that evening, so I went back downtown to the courthouse. When I peeked into the courtroom, Vernon Spencer and Doyle Proctor were sitting in the same places as when I'd left the day before. If they hadn't changed their clothes, I'd have sworn they'd been there all night. I went in to say hello to Georgia, and she informed me that the case was getting ready to go to the jury. If I was interested, she said, I could go inside and sit in on the final arguments.

I entered the courtroom and slipped onto one of the back benches beside some of the other spectators. The judge was droning on and on to the jury about the charge. I hadn't quite settled myself when, glancing at Vernon Spencer, he nodded at me. I nodded back and stared at him for a minute. I wondered if he was my late-night caller. He couldn't possibly know that I'd talked to the Newbolds.

The judge finally finished up and then announced that Doyle Proctor would argue first, and also, if he so chose, last. Doyle Proctor rose from his chair and approached the jury box. Just before he began, his eyes swept the courtroom and stopped on mine. His look was intense. Then it was over and he was doing his dog-and-pony-show for the jurors. I felt uneasy. What was that all about?

After the arguments were over and the jurors had filed from their box into the conference room, I turned to leave, to wait for Spencer in the hall. I was going to approach him from the angle of taking him to lunch. I felt a tug on my arm and turned back. It was Vernon Spencer.

"Miss Davis?"

"Mr. Spencer?" I held out my hand.

His grip was firm, his skin warm. "Did you want to see me about Elizabeth? I received a message from you yesterday."

"Yes. Could we go somewhere and talk?"

"How about lunch?"

"You took the words right out of my mouth."

He grinned, his even white teeth flashing at me. "Let me put my bag in the judge's office, and I'll be right with you."

I watched while he packed up his over-sized briefcase and headed toward where Georgia was. Doyle Proctor was in my line of vision. He, too, was packing up a briefcase. His eyes flickered toward me, but didn't stop to take a rest. Spencer came out and motioned at me to go out in the hall. He went through the far door and met me.

Taking me by the elbow, he guided me into the elevator and then out onto the street. I walked along with him, passing the time of day. It wasn't until we ended up underground at The Kabob House, a Greek place, with our food in front of us, that either of us broached the subject of Elizabeth Reynolds.

I liked him. Besides being warm and friendly and having a good handshake, he had a sense of humor.

"So what are you, an investigative reporter or something?"

I laughed. I'd never considered that type of job, though it was a thought.

"No. I have my own business in Houston. I used to be a probation officer. I used to be a lot of things. Anyway, I quit the county payroll and opened up shop. Believe it or not, I'm a licensed private investigator. We're also private process servers and do other things, such as social studies, legal research, and typing—whatever the market will bear."

"That's a novel thought. Except for TV, I've never known of a woman detective."

I smiled. "I know, and it's about time, don't you think?"

"Sure. So why are you up here asking about Elizabeth?"

I watched him carefully, to gauge his reaction to my next words. "She was murdered in Houston."

His eyes grew wide, and he expelled a gust of air, as if someone had unexpectedly punched him in the stomach.

I wasn't meaning to be callous and insensitive, but I was hungry, so while he was gathering his wits about him, I took an enormous bite of my pita sandwich. It tasted scrumptious. The filling was steamed broccoli and cauliflower, and fresh avocado, among other things.

"Oh, shit," he murmured, finally, more to himself than to me.

I continued eating and watching him, waiting for an appropriate time to say something. His eyes had a slightly overcast look, as if his sense had taken a short vacation. He seemed to have a lot on his mind; he'd temporarily forgotten I was there.

Eventually he focused on me again and asked, "Who hired you, Robert?"

"No. A man in Houston that she worked for."

"She wasn't practicing law down there."

I slurped my milk through a straw and swallowed. "Nope. Waiting tables."

"Jesus!" His brow wrinkled.

I nodded. "Quite a comedown."

"How'd it happen?"

"Strangled."

"Jesus!" he said again.

He looked somewhat upset, but not exactly as broken up about it as I thought he should be.

"We looked for her. You know about her disappearance?"

"Yeah. At least, I've been able to pretty much piece it together. What happened?"

"She just left. She was there one day and gone the next. No explanation to anyone. Robert was pretty devastated."

"And you?"

A thin veil seemed to drop over his face. If I hadn't been studying him, I wouldn't have seen it.

"I was in shock."

"You seem to have recovered nicely."

He reared back in his chair now—suspicious. "You mean my office?"

"Yes."

"I moved there because I didn't fit in with her people. I didn't belong. I'd been trying to tell Liz that for a long time. She just didn't want to hear it."

"How long were you two together?"

"Three years."

"That's a long time for someone to do something they don't want to do."

"Look, lady, I don't know what you're getting at, but Liz and I were close. Real close. I was going to split from her eventually, but it wasn't the easiest thing to do. She wanted to do a lot of charity work. I wanted to make money. Everytime I'd broach the subject of taking on a different kind of clientele, we'd have an argument. She was one of those people that could talk anyone into anything, you know what I mean? She should have been in sales; she'd have made a mint."

"How close is close?"

"Her kids were like my own. When Anne was smaller, she'd jump into my arms every time she saw me. She's too big, now. Catherine and I were buddies. I'd shoot straight with her. If she got any weird ideas, she'd bounce them off me. That's how close."

A likely story, I thought as I chewed.

Chapter 19

AFTER LUNCH, I WANDERED AROUND DOWNTOWN for awhile until it was time to drive out to the Reynolds place. When I drove up I spotted a brown-haired woman get into a car and drive away, wheels whirling on the gravel.

Mr. Reynolds invited me in, and this time the whole family deluged me. I was introduced to Anne, a tall, thin, athletic girl of fourteen, and Catherine, who I found out had just turned eighteen. She was indeed graduating from high school soon.

"The girls and I stayed home today," he said. "I told them about Elizabeth last night, and we've been trying to sort things out in our heads."

I smiled and nodded at them. They had seated me in the recliner and were gathered around me like they were going to perform an operation.

"How did my mother die, Miss Davis?" Catherine asked.

I glanced from her to the others. Talk about putting me on the spot. I didn't know whether I should give them the blow-by-blow or not; breaking bad news was never one of my duties in child welfare or the probation department. I decided to give them the police version. "She was found in her apartment one morning by her employer. She was late for work, and he went up to check on her. It's believed by the Houston Police Department that she was the victim of a serial killer."

"When was that?" Mr. Reynolds asked.

"How come the police didn't call us or something?" Anne asked. She was standing in front of me, sort of jumping around from one foot to the other. I got the impression that she was the real energetic sort. I was growing tired just watching her.

Catherine remained silent. I guess she caught on that I didn't really answer her question.

"It was Tuesday, a week ago, and they didn't call because she was calling herself Doris Jones. Remember I mentioned that to you yesterday, Mr. Reynolds?"

He nodded, his mouth turned down in a frown. "Isn't it a little unusual for someone like yourself to get involved in something like this?"

"Well, yes and no. The police are convinced that it was a serial killing, and when Carl, that's the man that owns the cafe she worked at—"

"What was she doing working at a cafe?" Anne asked. "She wasn't a lawyer anymore?"

"Anne," Mr. Reynolds said, "remember I told you after she disappeared that we checked out all the lawyers in the state and she wasn't practicing law? There were no listings anywhere for her."

"Oh, yeah."

"Let Miss Davis finish," Catherine said in a big-sisterish tone of voice.

I smiled at Catherine. She seemed the most aloof of the three. She was holding back. I knew about the letters, only she didn't know I knew. If I could just get her alone and see what she knew. The other two didn't seem to know or else they weren't letting me know yet that they knew.

"Go ahead, Miss Davis," Mr. Reynolds said.

"Well, it's only that Carl tried to tell them that he didn't think she was who she held herself out to be, but they didn't believe him, so he hired me to look into it. You see, Carl doesn't believe it was a serial killer. He thinks that she knew whoever it was." I was watching Mr. Reynolds, waiting for a reaction. There was none other than his eyebrows knitting together.

"So the police don't know you're up here?" he asked.

"They would've except when I tried to tell them, they wouldn't listen."

"Who would have done that to Mom?" Anne asked, her eyes welling up with tears.

I reached for her hand. It was soft and damp and warm except for a few places on her palm where there were calluses. I gave it a squeeze. "That's what I'm hoping to find out, Anne," I said.

The tears spilled out over her tanned cheeks. She swiped at them with her fingers.

"Come on, Anne," Catherine said. "Let's go into the kitchen and get a snack and let Miss Davis and Dad talk." She put her arm around her little sister's shoulders and led her out of the room.

Mr. Reynolds sat down adjacent to me on the sofa and shook his head. "You know, this whole thing has been so puzzling."

"I can imagine," I said. "Tell me, Mr. Reynolds, do you have any idea why she disappeared?"

He shook his head again. "None. I came home one day, and she was gone. She left a note saying that she didn't have any choice but to leave town, and not to worry, and that she'd come back as soon as she could. That was it."

"Do you know if she was in any kind of trouble?"

"No. She would have told me; I'm sure of it. I can't imagine anything that could be so bad that we couldn't have solved it. I thought for a while that she'd run off with someone else, but I couldn't really believe that. She loved the kids too much. I thought she loved me too much. We'd been through a lot together."

"Did you look for her? I mean, did you really look? Hire a private detective or anything."

"Yes. For a few months I went crazy with worry. I had this man, Barney Cline, and he helped me out, but he couldn't find her. He was expensive, and I couldn't afford him after a while."

"Things have been pretty tough both financially and emotionally, I guess."

He nodded and shifted his eyes away. He wiped them with the sleeve of his sports shirt. "Look, Miss Davis—"

"Mavis."

"Mavis. University professors don't earn that much. We went out and bought this big house when interest rates were high and prices were high, but Liz made good money so it didn't matter. We ran up a bunch of charge accounts for the furniture, and of course, we had all kinds of accounts for clothes, and we'd eat out all the time. You know how it is. The great American family is in greater debt than ever before."

I nodded.

"Well, when she left, we had very little savings. Some, but not much. And that was used up pretty quickly on Barney. I had trouble making the bills without her income. After I got over the upset, I've got to tell you, I was pretty damn mad at her for doing this to me. Anyway, Vem helped out for a while. Sort of buying out her share of the partnership."

"Vernon Spencer? He gave you money?"

"Yes. He said that he felt he owed it to us, because he was still receiving money in on some of her cases. You know, clients that paid by the month. So he gave me some money each month for about six months."

"How much?"

"About five hundred a month, give or take a little. If I couldn't make ends meet, I'd call him and he might send me an extra hundred or so. It helped pay some of the debts down to a reasonable level. The interest rates of nineteen and twenty percent on some of them were killing me."

"Didn't you find that odd?"

"What? That he sent us money?"

"Yes. Didn't that make you suspicious?" It made me suspicious. Why hadn't Spencer told me about that? He'd certainly had the opportunity.

"No. He said it would have been the same way if she had died. Shoot, if she'd died, I'd have been better off. At least I had life insurance on her. So, Vem said that he would have been obligated to sort of buy out her interest in the partnership, her share of the books and furniture, and the accounts. Anyway, I used that money to get the bills down, occasionally giving Barney a few dollars, and after I got to where I felt like I had my head above water, I would have used it to start searching for Elizabeth again, but then he quit sending it."

"Why?"

"Said he thought he was all paid up. He showed me some accounting. I wouldn't know the difference anyway. He would have loaned me some money, but I wouldn't have had any way of paying it back."

"So how long did Barney what's-his-name actually search for your wife?"

"Cline. A couple months, more or less."

"And he couldn't find out anything?"

"He found her car. She had sold it in Dallas for a few dollars and what was owed on it. We never could figure out how she left or if she even did leave this area, until later. We didn't even know if she was alive or dead for a long time."

"What do you mean? Did Cline find out where she went?" I could see that I was going to have to have a talk with that boy.

"No. About six months ago, I started receiving money from her."

"You did? Well what did she do, wire it, mail it, or what?"

"Mailed it to me."

"Did she write or anything?" I was hoping he knew about Catherine's letters and would tell me now.

"No. I would receive an envelope each month with no return address. They were postmarked Houston. They contained money orders, but each month they were different. I called the post office and asked them if there was any way they could tell me what part of Houston something came from, but they said that even stuff from a lot of small towns around Houston would be postmarked Houston."

"Didn't Barney go to Houston looking for her?"

"No. Where would he look? I wasn't going to waste money I didn't have paying him when I couldn't think of anything he could do that I couldn't. I went to the library and tried to find her in the new phone book, and I called directory assistance, but there was no listing. We had also checked with the state bar, but she apparently let her license lapse, so I knew she wasn't practicing law. At least, if she was, she wasn't doing it legally. I didn't think she was anyway, because we had put the word out and sent a picture around and if another lawyer had spotted her, I would have heard about it or else Vern would have."

"I wish she would have written to you or something." Hint, hint.

"Yeah, me too," he said dryly. "It was the weirdest thing. Nobody knew anything. It was as if someone had waved a magic wand over her head and made her disappear."

"What about credit cards? Didn't she charge on them after she left?"

"No. I found them on the kitchen counter together with most of the stuff that she would normally carry in her purse. You or the police didn't find her driver's license?"

"No. There was nothing in her apartment except a few things I discovered up in the attic crawl space, including that photograph I showed you yesterday."

"By the way, Mavis, did you say that her boss hired you to investigate her death?"

"Yeah, Carl Singleton."

"What did she do for him?"

"She was a waitress in his cafe."

He closed his eyes and shook his head. When he looked up again, he said, "What was she to him, Mavis?"

"He loved her, Mr. Reynolds, but I don't think they were lovers if that's what you mean."

"That's what I meant, yes. What's he like?"

"A nice guy, but definitely not her type. Believe me—there was nothing between them."

He sighed. "I wondered."

"And you? Was there anyone else for you?"

He looked up, surprise in his eyes. "Not really."

"Do you mind telling me who that woman was that I passed as I pulled up?"

"What? Oh. No one special. Madge Hennesey. She was Liz's best friend."

So that was Madge. I loved her name. I could empathize with someone labeled Madge. I smiled at Mr. Reynolds, but he couldn't know why. "I wish she would have stayed. I would have liked to meet her."

"She felt awkward about it, and she was pretty overwrought. Besides, she's just returned from a two-week vacation and has a lot of things to catch up on. She and another girl went on a cruise."

"Must be nice. Where'd they go?"

"South. Cancun, Cozumel, and someplace else. You'd have to ask her."

"I'd like to meet her and see if she knows anything that would be helpful. Do you think she'd mind?"

"No. I'll arrange it and call you."

I stood up and turned to leave. There wasn't much else I could get from him if he didn't know about Catherine's letters.

He walked me to the door. I hollered good-bye to the girls, and they hollered back from the kitchen. I stopped outside the door, remembering one more thing. "By the way, Mr. Reynolds. You mentioned life insurance. How much insurance was there on Elizabeth?"

"Two-hundred-and-fifty-thousand."

Chapter 20

"MAVIS DAVIS?" A LOUD, GRUFF VOICE inquired when I picked up the receiver. It didn't sound like the mystery caller of the year.

"Yes." I rubbed the sleep from my eyes, flipped on the bedside lamp, and squinted at my wristwatch. It was the witching hour.

"I need to talk to ya."

"Who's this?" I sat up in bed and pulled the covers up to my chin.

"Never mind who this is. I'll tell ya when you get here."

"Honey, I'm not going anywhere until I know who I'm talking to," I said. My stomach felt a bit queasy. I'm not sure if it was fear or the greasy dinner I'd eaten at the motel.

"All right. M'name's Willard, and I wanna talk to ya about Lawyer Reynolds," the deep voice said.

I was suddenly wide awake. "What is it you want?"

"To talk. I just said so, didn't I?"

"So talk already."

"Not over the phone. You gotta come here and meet me."

"My mother didn't raise any fools, Mr. Willard. If you've got something to say, say it."

"It's not Mr. Willard. Just Willard. I got some information for ya on Lawyer Reynolds. Ya want it or don't ya?"

"I do, I do, but you can't expect me to come out in the middle of the night to meet a stranger. I'm not crazy." Nervous, yes—crazy, no.

"Nothin's gonna happen to ya; just meet me. I can't stay on the phone too long. If ya don't wanna know, don't come. Otherwise, show up at the intersection of Main and Rosedale in an hour."

The phone clicked in my ear and then I got a dial tone. Maybe I was crazy, but I pulled on my jeans, a T-shirt, and tennis shoes and climbed into my Mustang. After studying the map, I headed toward downtown Fort Worth, which was the last place I wanted to be in the middle of the night.

When I reached Main and Rosedale, a big car flashed its lights at me and did a U-turn. I followed it to who knows where and finally, when it pulled over, so did I. We were in the middle of nowhere.

A huge man dressed all in black got out of the old Cadillac I'd been following and lumbered back toward me. I rechecked to be sure my doors were locked. My palms became sweaty.

He knocked on my window and I rolled it down about an inch so he could talk to me. "You Mavis Davis?"

"Uh-huh." I nodded vigorously.

"I'm Willard. You wanna get out of the car?"

No, I didn't. I looked back at him apprehensively. He was leaning down, speaking through the crack. I could no longer see his whole face, but his body I could see, and he was enormous—about the size of a black bear I'd once seen in a zoo. My heart was racing; then I realized how stupid I must look. And actually, when you get right down to it, the man probably could have ripped the car door right off its hinges if he so desired. What the heck, I thought, you only live once, and considering he hadn't threatened me or anything, I decided that it would only be polite if I got out.

I got out and immediately realized how helpless I'd be if he wasn't the friendly type. He didn't offer to shake hands or anything, which was fine with me, so I stood there waiting to hear what he had to say.

"I hear you're investigatin' on Lawyer Reynolds—that she's dead. Well, I'm here to tell ya that I didn't do it."

"Well, that's a relief," I said.

He cocked his head to one side and gave me an odd look. "What are you, a smart ass or somethin'?"

I was startled. Me and my big mouth. "Look, I'm sorry Mr. Willard."

"Thompson."

"What? Oh, Mr. Thompson. Right. I'm sorry if I was flippant; it's just that you get me out here in the middle of the night to tell me you didn't murder Elizabeth Reynolds, and I don't even know prior to this that you exist. What do you expect me to say?"

"Huh. I thought you'd already be zeroing in on me, that someone would've tipped you off that I was out of the joint, and you'd figure I done it. I just wanted to tell ya that I didn't." He was staring down at me from where he stood on the pavement, his dark eyes unfathomable in the dim streetlights. I was not comforted by the knowledge that he'd just gotten out of the "joint."

"Why would I have thought you killed her?"

"'Cause I would've if I'd know where she was. She stole my dope before she disappeared."

He could have knocked me over with a feather. I mean it. This was the first I'd heard about dope. I was beginning to feel like one. A dope, I mean. "Yes, well, Mr. Thompson, this is all news to me. I didn't know she was a doper."

"She didn't use it; she sold it."

Well, faint and fall out. I stared hard at the man. "Are you sure we're talking about the same woman?"

"Yeah. Elizabeth A. Reynolds. She was my lawyer for years."

"Okay. So why do you think she stole your dope? What was it anyway, pot?"

"Coke. And I don't think it. I know it. I've had a year to figure it out, and she took it all right, and then she split, 'cause she knew if she hung around that I'd come after her when I got out."

"But that doesn't make any sense, Mr. Thompson. She could have hung around at least another eleven months if you were in Huntsville in the penitentiary."

"I wasn't there when she left. I was in the local slammer. Look. This is the way it was. It took me a long time, but now I got it all figured out." He started ticking off reasons on his fingers. "She found out that I was selling dope to kids, right? Then she set me up for a fall. I get picked up, but I'm not holding much. Only I got a history. I call her, but I ain't got no bread, so I tell her that if she'll get me out of jail on bond, that I'll get the bread. She says she don't do bonds and can't get me out, when she really don't mean for me to get out at all, but I don't know that. So finally, I tell her that if she'll get my dope, she can sell it and get the bread and get me out and pay herself to fix up my case. So I tell her where it is. It was a lot, too. Man, I bet she was living like a princess. Anyhow, instead of getting me out, she gets my dope and skips. See why I would've wasted her if I caught up to her?"

I'm totally flabbergasted. "Why did you think that she'd sell the dope for you and get you out?"

"Ya hear a lot in the slammer. It was like, you know, she pretended she wanted to help them people, but she was really usin' 'em. There was this setup with a DA, see."

"Yeah? What kind of setup?"

"I'm not clear on that, yet, but I'm workin' on it. I heard she'd set people up to get busted."

"What? You mean she'd inform on her own clients?"

"Yeah, well, some people will do anything for a few bucks."

"You're kidding." She would have had to be out of her mind to do that. No wonder she'd been killed.

"Hey, I don't know for sure, but it seemed thataway. All I know is, when I told her where my dope was, she split, but I swear I didn't kill her, though I would've. I bet she was having a great time with my money."

"Would it surprise you to know that Mrs. Reynolds was living in abject poverty when she was killed?"

"Huh?"

"She was poor, Mr. Thompson. Was waiting tables in a slummy cafe in Houston."

"That don't make no sense when she stole my dope."

"Maybe she didn't steal it. Maybe it was just a coincidence that she disappeared around the time that your dope was taken."

"I ain't buyin' that. Nobody else knew where I put it. She was the only one. Except …"

"Except who, Mr. Thompson?"

"Nah. Nobody. I left this kinda-coded message with her secretary, see, but I don't think her secretary would've know what it meant. It had to be Lawyer Reynolds."

A car drove by slowly just then, and Willard glanced over at it nervously. "I gotta go, lady."

"Wait, I have some more questions for you."

"Can't wait," he said, looking all around, as if expecting someone.

"How will I get in contact with you if I need to talk to you again?"

"I'll call ya. Don't tell nobody I talked to ya, okay?"

"Okay, Mr. Thompson. Look, I'm sorry I smarted off earlier. I really do appreciate your coming forward with this information."

He nodded at me and started backing toward his car.

Say, Mr. Thompson, how'd you know about me? How'd you know where to find me?"

"Fort Worth is a small town, lady," he said. "I gotta go." And he got into his worn Cadillac, started it up, and drove off, leaving me standing in the street God knows where, about as confused as I had ever been in my whole life. I watched after him, memorizing his license number, and then climbed back into my car. I drove around for a while until I found a highway I recognized and then used the map to get back to my motel.

When I got back, the little red light was lit up on my phone, so I called the office for the message. Catherine Reynolds had called and left a message that she'd call back. I slept until then. She wanted to meet with me the following day right after school, and would I go to the Candleglow Inn at three-thirty? I said I would and went back to sleep. It was by that time three-thirty in the morning and although I had a lot to think about, I didn't have the energy to do the thinking.

Chapter 21

FIRST THING THE NEXT DAY, I went back to Spencer's office and cornered him.

The ice maiden led me to his private office upstairs from the reception area. It was more of a suite than an office. I found him sitting in an all-leather armchair adjacent to a matching sofa. On the opposite side of the room was his hand-carved teak desk, adorned with fresh flowers in a Waterford crystal vase, and velvet-covered client chairs. The walls held original oil paintings, his license, and his law school diploma in $300 frames.

"Why didn't you tell me that you subsidized the Reynolds' family after Elizabeth's disappearance?" I demanded rudely as soon as the door closed behind the clone.

He was smooth, I'll give him that. I was more suspicious of him than ever, and he must have known it, but he sat back calmly in his chair, his shirt sleeves rolled up, his silk tie knotted loosely at his throat, a legal pad in his lap, a gold pen in hand, some law books on the end table beside his chair, and smiled at me. Well, little did he know that I wasn't having any that day.

"I didn't see that it was of any importance, Miss Davis. Please, sit down. Get comfortable."

I remained standing. "Why did you do it? And where did you get the money to give to them and buy all this, too?"

"You don't understand, Miss Davis. I owed it to Robert. It was his fair share of Liz's and my partnership. I knew he'd be having hard times with Liz gone. Shoot, she brought in at least twice as much money as he did. All I did was buy him out on the installment plan."

"Yeah, and quit paying when you found out that he had an investigator hunting for her."

He slouched back into his chair, foot up on the coffee table. "That's ridiculous. I knew all along that he had a detective looking for her. Why would I cut him off after so many months?"

"Maybe you thought he was getting close to finding her."

"Don't be stupid. I simply calculated how much it would take to buy out her share of the library and the few pieces of furniture that I wanted to bring with me, and believe me, there was hardly a thing I wanted, and sent him a check each month. If there was an installment payment from one of her clients, I'd forward that, too. It wasn't that much money, but Robert needed it."

"Sure fella."

"What am I, a suspect or something?" He chuckled, but his eyes flashed angrily.

"I don't know yet, Mr. Spencer."

"You think I killed her? Why would I do that? I loved her. She was like a sister, or even a mother, to me."

"Who do you think killed her?"

"How would I know? Maybe it was a serial killer like the police in Houston think."

"How did you know that?"

"You must have told me. I don't know."

"I didn't. Who've you been talking to?"

"Robert. Is that a crime? We talk all the time. If you really want someone with a motive, why don't you look at him? He had that large life-insurance policy on her and has a girlfriend that likes him a lot." He grinned at me, his eyes lighting up. I didn't trust him. He was probably trying to get the heat off himself.

"Who's that?"

"Girl, don't you know anything? Madge Hennesey."

"I thought she was Elizabeth's best friend."

"Some best friend. She didn't wait five minutes to move in on Liz's territory. There probably hasn't been a day go by that she hasn't been over there giving comfort to Robert."

I thought about that. Was that what Catherine wanted to tell her mother? Robert had said there wasn't anybody significant. Why would he lie about it? It would be perfectly normal for a man to want someone else after a long year of loneliness. Could he have found out where she was and killed her for the insurance money?

"Were the premiums still being paid on the life insurance, Mr. Spencer?"

"I wouldn't know about that. They used to be drawn on the office account, but I put a stop to that after she left. You'd have to ask Robert, but I would think so." He was still smiling, but it wasn't a friendly sort of smile.

"Who was the insurance carrier?"

"National Life, Dallas. They're in the book."

I flipped open my spiral and wrote that down. "I'll call them."

"You do that, lady. Any more questions? I've got a lot of catching up to do. I was in trial, remember?"

"Yeah. What kind of cases was Elizabeth handling when y'all were partners?"

"Mostly family and criminal, a little personal injury."

"Did she ever talk to you about anyone who would be especially angry over the way she had handled a case?"

"One or two, but that was a year ago. Those people wouldn't have any more way of knowing where she was living than I would."

"Did she handle many drug cases?" I was watching him carefully now, trying to gauge his reaction. I got what I expected. His face turned a paler shade of brown, but he managed not to flinch.

"Not many. Why do you ask?"

"Do you?"

I saw tiny beads of sweat begin to form on his upper lip. His eyes stared into mine, unwavering. "You know I do. You sat through my final argument on one yesterday."

"Oh, right." My turn to grin. I turned and grabbed the doorknob. "Thanks a lot, Vern. Be talking to you." And I got the heck out of there.

* * *

"Barney Cline Detective Agency," a high-pitched voice said into the phone. I was calling from the ground floor of the criminal courts building where I had come to do some homework.

"Is Mr. Cline there?"

"Yes ma'am, hang on," the voice said. I could picture some skinny blond chick with a teased-up hairdo and a fingernail file in her hand.

"Cline," came a second voice, a tenor.

"Mr. Cline, my name is Mavis Davis. I'm looking into Elizabeth Reynolds' disappearance, and I understand that you did a search for Mr. Reynolds."

"That's true. What's your angle?"

"She's dead, and I'm trying to find out who killed her."

"Yeah? Well, I can't help you there, Miss." There wasn't even a sharp intake of breath from his end. He was a cold so-and-so.

"Well, I figured that, but you must have found out a lot about her when you were working for Mr. Reynolds, and I wondered if you discovered whether she had any known enemies."

"Nope."

"Do you know exactly what kind of cases she was working on when she disappeared?"

"Little of everything, I guess. Most of these small law offices, that's what they handle, nothing real big. I can't remember anything specific."

"Criminal?"

"Yeah, some of that, drugs, burglary, juvenile stuff. I checked with the courthouse, and they had some of those sheets with her name listed on it. I also talked to her secretary. Say, you might talk to her. She could be right helpful."

"You wouldn't happen to know her name, would you? She's not with Mr. Spencer anymore."

"Sorry. Ask Spencer."

"I don't want to do that."

"He a suspect? Never did trust that nig—black son-of-a-bitch."

I grimaced. "I wouldn't say he's a suspect, and I wouldn't say he isn't either, but there's just something about him, you know what I mean?"

"Yeah, there's something funny about him. Sure came up in the world after she left. Not that they were doin' so bad before, but you couldn't tell it from the trappings. You go by the old office?"

"Yes."

"Then you know what I mean. Some rich fella is buying up a bunch of property now and is gonna revamp it and get richer I hear."

"So you don't have any notes on the name of the old secretary?"

"Never take many notes and never save 'em after I get through with a case. Call Mr. Reynolds; he'll know."

"Well, thanks a lot. You've been a great help."

I went upstairs to the district clerk's office and requested Willard Thompson's file. I wanted to verify his statements.

Boy, was it a surprise. The docket sheet had listed Elizabeth Reynolds as the attorney of record, but then her name had been crossed out and replaced with Vernon Spencer's.

I poured over the file. He had originally been charged with possession of a Controlled Substance, two counts. One was for phenmetrazine and the other for cocaine. There was an enhancement for a prior conviction, so he could have gone up for a long time, but the phenmetrazine charge and the enhancement were dropped. He had pleaded guilty to a third-degree felony and been sentenced to ten years in the Texas Department of Corrections with credit for time served in the county jail.

And he had told me that he'd just gotten out. I checked the date of the plea, and, with his jail-time credit, he'd done a total of a tad over a year. Our great legal system.

I scanned the plea papers for the name of the prosecutor. I wondered if the man that signed the papers had been the one Thompson had thought would prosecute the case. I wondered if there was any truth to the rumor that Elizabeth set up her clients for a fall. The name at the bottom of the page, the prosecutor, was Doyle Proctor, the same one that had been in trial the last few weeks on the drug case opposite Vernon Spencer.

I closed the file and went next door looking for Doyle Proctor. He wasn't in, so I left a card with my motel number on it. I was anxious to pass the time of day with him. Maybe he could shed some light on the case. Also, to be on the safe side, I was just thinking that it wouldn't hurt to let law enforcement know what I was doing in Fort Worth.

Down on the ground floor, again, I called Mr. Reynolds at his office and procured the name of the old secretary. While I was on the phone, he told me that Madge wanted to meet me for lunch if I would call her and set it up. I did. Then I set about calling law firms, beginning with the first office listed in the yellow pages. Boy were my fingers tired when I found her.

"Tammy Bradley?" I asked when the receptionist connected me with her.

"Yes. Who's this?"

"You don't know me, Miss Bradley, but my name is Mavis Davis. I'm looking into the death of Elizabeth Reynolds."

Gasp. Sputter. Sniffle.

"Miss Bradley? I'm sorry. I shouldn't have broken it to you that way. Are you okay?"

No response.

"Miss Bradley? Are you there? I'd like to meet with you, if you don't mind. I have some questions I'd like to ask you."

"I guess they found her after all," she said in a breathy whisper.

Chapter 22

TAMMY BRADLEY WAS CRYING AND SO incoherent that I couldn't make much sense out of what she was saying. Before hanging up, I managed to get her to agree to meet me for lunch the following day. She definitely knew something, and I wanted to find out what that something was.

I went to my lunch date with Madge Hennesey. We met down in the Tandy Center, at the Spud 'N Salad. The tunnel seemed to be the most popular eatery around.

Madge was of medium height. Her backside, which I noticed while we were standing in line for our food, looked as if she d been run over by a steamroller. She had just about the widest hips and smallest behind of anyone I'd ever known. She wasn't fat. To the contrary, she was skinny, and she was the first woman I'd seen in a long time that had a chest flatter than mine. I liked her immediately. Her blue eyes were so large that they seemed about the size of silver dollars. Her turned up, almost bulbless, little nose was peeling from a recent sunburn. She had skinny lips and movie-star cheekbones. She wore her straight brown hair with bangs, and it was cropped off at chin length. Looking at her made me think of Prince Valiant in the comic strips, minus a sheath of arrows.

She was wearing a white short-sleeved blouse, a man's necktie, and a navy skirt that fell below her knees. Her clothes resembled a parochial-school uniform. She found me waiting at a table and called to me as if we were long-lost friends. She bubbled over with friendliness and shook my hand so tightly that I thought she was going to fracture my metacarpals.

"Mavis Davis. What a name!" She said and laughed as she released my hand. Her laugh came from deep down inside her, and I couldn't help but laugh with her.

"Our mothers didn't know the bounds of cruelty, did they?"

"What? Oh, you mean my name." She laughed again. It was contagious. "I'm constantly getting kidded about that lady on the TV commercials."

"I sympathize with you."

"And you've got double trouble, with that red hair. Anybody ever call you Red?"

"Not lately. I'd probably shoot them if they did. If I owned a gun."

Laughter again. "You're funny, Mavis. Guess that's a defensive measure, huh?"

"Yeah. That's me. A laugh a minute. I hate to get down to serious business, Madge, but why don't we get our lunch and then we can talk about Elizabeth Reynolds."

She sobered up then, a frown tugging at the corners of her mouth. "Okay."

I followed her into a food line, chatting about one thing and another. I found out that she was an officer at a downtown bank.

She had been there for almost sixteen years, starting as a line teller, and, with banking courses at Tarrant County Junior College, had worked her way up. She was now an assistant vice-president in installment loans.

"How long did you know Elizabeth?" I asked when we were situated back at the table. She had an enormous baked potato with the works, and a salad almost as tall as Mount Everest, and looked from it to me, as if she was more interested in eating than talking.

"Since she was pregnant with Anne." Then she quickly broke up her potato and stuffed about a fifth of it into her mouth, sour cream oozing from her lips.

"How did you meet her?" I could see there would be a handsome interval while she chewed and swallowed. I took a bite of mine while I waited.

Finally, she answered. "She was taking one or two courses at night while Robert was going to school full-time. We had a class together, and we'd stand out in the hall during the break and smoke. That was before I really got on my health kick, but I remember that I told her she shouldn't smoke when she was pregnant." She jammed a mound of salad in as soon as the words came out.

"What health kick?" I asked as I watched her eat.

She grinned. "I work out. I lift weights and run. It doesn't seem to matter what I eat. I never put on an ounce. I'm not into health foods, but I quit smoking a long time ago, and I'm as healthy as a horse."

I was jealous. If I ate all the time the way I had been eating the last few days, and the way she was eating today, I'd look like the Goodyear blimp.

"So you and Elizabeth got to be friends at college?"

She nodded. "I was going through my first divorce and because of Roger I didn't have many friends. He drove them all away. I started hanging around Elizabeth. I liked her. She seemed to be so sophisticated, sort of, and I was the awkward, clumsy type. She was happy all the time, even though she and Robert were having tough times while they were in school."

"Did you stay friends when they moved down to Austin?"

"Oh, you know about that? Yeah. I would drive down there for weekends every once in a while. We drifted apart after a while, and I remarried while she was gone, but by the time they moved back, I was on the brink of divorce again. After a while, we were as close as ever." She smiled.

"How often did you two see each other?"

"All the time. I was over at their house practically daily. We'd eat dinner together, and I'd help her with the kids. Those kids are great. Or I'd help Robert if Elizabeth was at work. She worked a lot of long hours after she and Vern set up their practice. Sometimes she wouldn't come home until way after I'd put the kids to bed."

"You weren't married; you were divorced by then?"

"Yeah. Joel and I split about five years or so ago, I think. He was a real prick."

"Do you have kids, Madge?"

"Nah. I never wanted any with either of my husbands. Well, Roger and I were only married for about eighteen months. I knew right away that I'd made a mistake with him; it just took me that long to get out of it. And Joel, well, he was a drinker. I knew that when I married him, but I didn't know how bad it was. He'd get real mean." She laughed again. "He was one mean son-of-a-bitch, that boy was."

"That's tough."

"Yeah. What about you? You got any kids? You married?"

"No to both questions. I'm too independent, I guess."

She shrugged her shoulders. "I know what you mean."

"So tell me, how much did you know about the actual workings of Elizabeth's law practice? Did she confide in you?"

Her eyes shifted down toward her food, and she took another bite of her potato, chewing thoughtfully before answering. "Some," she said.

"Can you think of any reason that would cause her to disappear like she did?"

"You want to know how many hours I've thought that one over? I wish I did. You know, it was crazy. The way she did it, I mean. She'd been working along as usual and then suddenly one day she was gone. She left Robert. She left the girls. I couldn't believe it. How could she have done it?"

"Do you know what she was working on at the time?"

"Some criminal, some divorce. You know, the usual kind of stuff. No, she was probably doing more criminal than usual. She'd got a lot of criminal court appointments in the months just before that, and Vernon was doing a whole lot of criminal work—more than Elizabeth ever wanted them to take in."

"Did they have any disagreements that you know of?"

"You mean, did she and Vern fight about it?"

I nodded. "Yes. Did they get along?"

"Elizabeth wasn't a fighter; she was a talker. She had talked Vernon Spencer into coming up here to work with the inner city youth and the poor. She told him that they could do other things, but that the little people of Fort Worth needed someone to be on their side. She promised him that there would be a lot of time left over for making money as well."

"So how did it actually work out?"

"I think he came because he was black." She slurped at her lemonade. "Not because he wanted to help the blacks, you understand, but because there aren't many opportunities for black lawyers. I mean, they can make, what do you call it, law review and stuff like that; they can excel in law school, win oratory awards, and all that stuff, but the big firms with the big money still aren't going to hire them because of their race.

"Vern wasn't any different, and I think he did excel. So did Elizabeth, but she wasn't interested in making the really big bucks; she just wanted to make a comfortable living, which she did—they both did—and she wanted to help the people she grew up around."

"That's what I heard the other day," I said.

"Yeah? From who, Robert?"

"The Newbolds."

"Those old people that own the drugstore. I've met them. They're real sweet people." She smiled across the table at me. "Anyway, I think that Vern and Elizabeth got to be friends and she persuaded him to come up here, made him a bunch of promises, but the money didn't come in fast enough for him. He didn't give a damn about the people; he didn't grow up here. She told me that he was taking on more and more criminal work—making a big name for himself as a criminal attorney. She didn't like that, because he was representing some of the same people that were committing crimes and dealing drugs right in that neighborhood."

"So they weren't getting along?" I was growing more and more confused. Who was telling the truth? Was Elizabeth into dope or wasn't she? Did Vernon Spencer get rid of her, or didn't he?

"No, but like I said, Elizabeth wouldn't have had fights with him. As a matter of fact, I think she was just going to pull up stakes, leave him. She found out the hard way that she couldn't save all those people by herself. She told me, and this was not too long before she disappeared, that she was talking with some large law firm that did personal injury. She was thinking of going to work for them if they'd let her continue to do a few hours work each week for her people."

"You couldn't give me the name of that firm, could you?"

She shook her head. "No, I'm sorry. Tammy might know, or else Robert."

"Tammy Bradley? Her secretary?"

"Yeah. Why, do you know her?"

"No, but I'm supposed to have lunch with her tomorrow."

"They were pretty tight, Mavis, but if she knows anything about why Elizabeth left, she's not telling. Everybody, and I mean everybody, quizzed her about it."

"Why isn't she working for Spencer anymore, do you know?"

"Not really. They didn't get along, I know that. He's a real moody kind of person, and I don't think she could take the pressure, but I don't know if that's why she left."

"I wonder if she's ever confided in Robert."

"Why would she do that?" Her face got an odd look on it, like she was alarmed. "I don't think so, he'd have told me."

"You and he are pretty close, aren't you?" I watched as she sat up straighter.

"Why do you say that?"

"Vernon Spencer said that. I didn't."

"We're friends, that's all." Suddenly the bubbliness was gone, and her eyes got a veiled look. The skin on her face grew taut. "I'm like a surrogate mother to the girls. Shoot, since Elizabeth became a lawyer, I've probably been more of a mother to them than she ever was. For the last year I've been the only mother they've known, the only female role model in their lives. You can't count Mrs. Newbold. She mostly just calls them on the phone."

"I'm sorry if I offended you, Madge. I have to follow up on everything I'm told."

"What else did Vern say? Did he tell you that I'm over at Robert's house every day? Did he tell you that I cook for them a lot and clean and help out any way I can? That bastard! He's just trying to make trouble, that's all. The most he did for Robert was send a few dollars. Where was he when Robert and Catherine and Anne needed someone to lean on?"

I quickly changed the subject. "Mr. Reynolds tells me that you just got back from vacation, that you took a cruise."

"So?" She really had her back up.

"So how was it? I've always wanted to go on a cruise ship. Where all did you go?"

She looked at me before answering, a funny little glint in her eye. Then she relaxed and everything seemed to be all right again.

"It was great. We saved all year to go. We flew to Miami and then caught the ship. Some days were spent at sea, but we stopped at Cancun, Cozumel, Grand Cayman, and then this private island. There was a beach party there. I got sunburned as you can see." She was laughing again. Everything was fine.

"Did you go snorkeling?"

"Yeah. They have this team of guys that take you. Some of them were real hunks, too. We got to see a sunken airplane. I think that was in Cozumel. I didn't stay the whole time because I wanted to go shopping."

"It sounds really wonderful. I'm dying to go on one. What cruise line was it?"

"N.C.L. Norwegian. The captain had the greatest accent." She laughed.

"So you'd recommend it, huh?"

"You bet. The worst thing about it was that it was too short. You don't get to stay in any one port of call more than a day, but I tell you, they treat you like royalty on the ship. You can eat all you want, and work out, and get a massage, and lay in the sun, and they'll bring the drinks right to you."

"Boy, it sounds great. Were there a lot of single guys? I have a friend that wants to go on one, but she wants to meet guys."

"How old is she?"

"Thirty-four, why?"

"'Cuz there's lots of young guys, but no one around our age. Tell her if she goes, to go for the fun of the cruise, not to look for guys. Unfortunately, most of the people our age were married."

"Well, I'd still like to go. Maybe I could save up for it, too."

"Look, Mavis. I've got to get back. If there's anything else I can tell you, call me, okay? And I'm sorry I got mad. Vern can get to me, you know?"

I nodded, and stood up with her. She held out her hand, and I was hesitant to take it, but I did. No bones cracked, but I expected to see bruises the next day.

Chapter 23

AFTER MADGE LEFT, I FOUND A phone book, got the address of the Candleglow Inn, then stopped back by the courthouse to see Doyle Proctor again. He still wasn't there, so I drove out to Arlington.

The Candleglow Inn was a run-down little restaurant which, I discovered later, was lit only with candles. I wondered if the food was so questionable that the management didn't want the customers to be able to see it clearly.

I waited outside in the near-vacant parking lot until Catherine came tearing up in her car. She waved at me and shut off the engine. She was dressed in slacks and a couple of layers of shirts belted at the waist, as was the style for kids other than Candy.

Catherine requested a corner booth and ordered a couple of beers for us. I must have shown mild surprise because she explained that it was one of the few places that didn't check ID cards when the drinking age in Texas was moved back up to twenty-one.

I studied the girl while we waited for our beers. She was nervous and fidgeted with the place mat, her dark-blue eyes casting about for some place to rest. The candlelight cast a warm glow on her face that only emphasized her youth. She wore almost no makeup that day; her complexion clear and smooth, there was nothing for her to cover up.

When the waitress brought the frosted mugs, I took a big gulp and smiled at Catherine. I wanted her to be at ease, to trust me. I knew it must have taken a lot of courage for her to call me.

"So how was school today?" I asked as I lit a cigarette and tried to strike an informal posture in the booth.

"The same," she answered, her eyes still flitting from place to place. "We're checking in books, getting ready for finals."

"Are you excited about graduation? I bet you wish your mother could have been here for it."

Her eyes stopped, resting on mine. She spoke hesitantly. "How much do you know, Miss Davis?"

"Mavis. And I don't know nearly as much as I need to."

"You've read my letters?"

"Two of them. Where did you send them?" I tried to be serious and calm, so I wouldn't scare her off.

"Care of general delivery in Dickinson."

I nodded. It made sense. It was near the bank, but far enough away from the cafe that no one would know.

"She called me a couple of weeks after she'd gone and told me where to write. She said she hated that she'd had to leave that way, but that it was for our protection, and it couldn't be any other way." Catherine's mouth turned down grimly.

"Did she tell you why she had to leave, Catherine?"

She shook her head slowly from side to side. "She wouldn't. I tried. I asked her many times, but she said I'd be in danger if I knew the reason. She said she'd come back when it was safe, but she didn't know when that would be." She took a swallow of her beer, and then choked on it, as if she couldn't get it past a lump in her throat.

I waited for her to quit coughing and then prodded further. "Did she write to you, too?"

"No. I'd write her every week or every two weeks, and she'd call me once a month usually. It would always be on a Monday, so every Monday I'd wait by the phone after school before Dad came home. If she didn't call by four-thirty, I'd know she wasn't going to."

"She never spoke to your dad?"

"No, and I didn't tell him about the calls either. She made me promise. She said if I told Dad or Anne or anyone else, that she'd stop. She told me once that she felt real guilty even calling me, but that she couldn't help it, that she had to have some contact with us. I was always real good at keeping secrets, Mavis, and Mom knew that. Besides, we were real close. We always have been. Before she left, when she was working all those long hours after she and Vernon went into business together, I would call her when I got home from school and we'd talk. Even if she had a client-in her office, she'd stop what she was doing, and we'd talk for five or ten minutes."

I shook my head at her. "It doesn't make sense to me that she wouldn't talk to your father."

"I know. I thought she was afraid of him at first, though I couldn't figure out why. They never fought, and I thought she really loved him. I tried to get her to talk to him, but I think she couldn't bear it, you know? Like he'd try to talk her into coming home—and she always insisted that she couldn't come home until her problem was solved."

"Surely in all this time she said something to you to indicate what this was all about?"

Catherine shook her head again. "No. She didn't. I swear. Every time I'd ask her, she'd say she couldn't tell me. I've thought and thought about it. The only thing she ever said, and I was hoping that you could make something out of this, was that she had some protection and until she could figure out what to do with it, she'd have to stay away."

Boy, what a mess. I studied Catherine's face while I thought about it. The waitress came and I ordered two more beers.

"Did she ever indicate if anyone else knew about this protection?"

"No. I'm sorry. I want to help, but she wouldn't talk about it. Wait—yes. One time she said that she thought help wasn't far away. That's why I thought she'd be able to come home soon."

"But she didn't say who it was?" I asked.

"Uh-uh. Not even a hint." She watched me while she took another sip.

"She didn't mention Vernon Spencer or Madge Hennesey?"

Again she shook her head. "Not except to ask how they were."

"What do you know about Vernon Spencer, Catherine?"

The girl stared at me and her eyes took on a more serious cast. "Now that you mention it, Mavis, not much. He started coming around in Austin when I was younger. He and Mom would study together. He was very poor. I heard him once talk about how rich we were compared to his family, when I didn't think we had anything at all. Mom wouldn't buy me a lot of the things I wanted back then." She glanced down at the table. "She said we couldn't afford it."

"You never overheard Spencer talking about his personal life or anything like that?" It occurred to me that I knew very little about the man, or for that matter, Madge, either.

She shook her head. "Just joking about how he couldn't wait to get out of law school and start making lots of money."

Well, it appeared he'd met his goal. "Did he ever bring any girls over?"

"Nope. Not in Austin or here."

"What about his family. Where's he from?"

She shrugged.

"Was he just secretive?"

"I don't know. Mom probably knew a lot more about him than we did."

"Yeah," I said. "Only we can't ask your mom."

Catherine sighed.

"What about Madge? What are your first memories of her?"

"I was around five or six, I think. She came to dinner. Before that I heard Mom telling Daddy about her."

"Did you like her then?"

She gave me an odd look. "Yeah, I guess I did. She's always been real sweet to me. Overly sweet—gushy—at times. She'd pinch my cheek and tell me how cute I was."

"I know what you mean. I have a hard time with people like that sometimes, don't you?"

"Yeah," she said and smiled. "A real hard time."

"You know anything about her personal life—where she's from or what her husbands were like?"

Catherine's brow wrinkled. "Grand Prairie, I think. Yeah, she went to a class reunion there. And yes, I met Roger when I was little. He always smelled bad and he would hug me. Yuck."

"What about the second one, Joel?"

"I never met him. Mother didn't either, but she hated him for making Madge lose the baby."

Madge must have "overlooked" telling me about the baby. I'm afraid I didn't disguise my surprise very well.

"No one told you about Madge losing her baby?" Catherine asked in response to, I'm sure, the bizarre expression on my face.

"I guess no one thought it was important," I said.

"Well, it was a long time ago. While we lived in Austin."

"I'm surprised you remember it then."

"I was thirteen, I think. Madge came down to see us when she was showing. She was probably four-or five-months pregnant."

"Oh."

"The next time, though, she wasn't pregnant and didn't have a baby with her, so I asked Mom."

"So what happened?"

She made an ugly face. "Joel beat her up and the baby was born dead." Her face grew melancholy.

When Madge said he was mean, she wasn't kidding. "Sad. Poor Madge. What happened to her husband?"

"I'm not sure. I think he got arrested, but after that, I don't know. Mom thought I was too young to understand, but I saw stuff like that on TV all the time."

"That's really a tearjerker."

"Yeah. I felt real sorry for Madge."

"That didn't make you like her any better, though, did it?"

"What do you mean?"

"Well, you're not crazy about her, are you?"

Catherine was scratching the frosting on the side of the beer mug.

"Catherine."

She shook her head once more.

"Did your mom know how you felt?"

"No. I didn't always feel that way."

"Come on, Catherine," I leaned in toward her. "Didn't you tell her about Madge and your father?"

She rolled her eyes and shifted in her seat uncomfortably. "How did you know about that?"

"I know."

"I guess I did mention to her that Madge was coming over all the time, Mavis, but it didn't seem real serious until recently. I wanted to talk to her about it some more, but I never got the chance. She didn't call me this month. I wrote to her and told her to call me, but she never did."

"What happened recently that made you think it was more serious?"

"Madge decided we should have a heart-to-heart," she said, her tone rich in sarcasm and anger.

"Yeah? What'd she say?"

Catherine sighed dramatically. "That she loved Dad and she thought he loved her and that she loved us, Anne and me, and that she hoped I didn't mind. She wanted to get married and would I not make it difficult for her, that Dad was lonely. All that kind of junk."

"I take it that you didn't approve."

"Of course not!" Her face was flushed now.

"Did you tell Madge?"

"Not in so many words, but she knows. She would tell Dad that she knew I would always be hoping for Mother's return. And I was. I kept telling him that I just knew she'd be coming back soon. Dad was really caught in the middle. He didn't know what to do. I knew he was lonely and that he cared about Madge, but not in the same way as for Mother. Madge had talked to him about getting a divorce or seeing a lawyer about having Mother declared dead." She frowned and leaned her chin on her elbow. "I guess he doesn't have to now, does he?"

"Did he before?"

"I don't know. He hadn't been discussing it with me much recently. I was afraid he was weakening; that's why I wanted to talk to Mother so badly. If she would have just come home."

"If we just knew why she couldn't."

We sat there looking at one another, both thinking our "if onlys." After a few minutes, Catherine said she had to leave. If she didn't get home soon, there'd be questions.

I paid for the beer and walked to Catherine's car with her, promising I'd be in touch.

After she left, I drove back to my room to freshen up for dinner. I wanted to get an early bite and then phone home. I had been feeling guilty about not talking to my favorite reporter, Fred Elliot, after we had made a deal, and then, too, I wanted to get the latest from Margaret.

I parked my Mustang, went into the motel office to get a newspaper, and then went to my room. I was scanning the front page as I put my key in the lock, not paying attention, like an idiot, and when I stepped through the door, I was clobbered on the back of the head.

I awoke seeing the fibers of the carpet from close range. I could smell that powdery stuff the maid sprinkled on the carpet before vacuuming. It had an aroma like roses and made me want to puke. My head was throbbing. Before I gathered myself up off the floor, I wiggled all my limbs to see if they still worked. They did.

I pulled myself up on the edge of the bed so I could get my bearings. The bedclothes were all in a pile. I glanced around the room. It was a mess. My suitcase was spread open on the floor. The dresser drawers had been ransacked, even the one with my dirty, smelly clothes in it. Half of them were hanging out; the other half had been dumped on the floor. Next to where I had been lying was my briefcase, the contents scattered. I was sure that my purse would have been stolen, but it was still there. The contents had been poured out over a wide area, but when I checked it, nothing was missing.

I made a determined effort to get to the phone. It wasn't easy. Each step caused a throbbing sensation throughout my brain. I called the police. I was scared. It was that simple. I didn't know what it was that whoever was looking for, but I hoped that it had been found. I did know that I was going to make many phone calls that night. If someone was going to cause me bodily injury, I wanted to be sure that the right people were apprised of the situation.

Chapter 24

"FRED, IT'S ME, MAVIS," I SAID into the phone after the Fort Worth police had gone.

"You bitch! Where in the hell have you been? What happened to your promise to keep in touch?" he said in a half-friendly tone.

"I fully deserve your wrath, Fred. I admit it. I apologize for not calling you sooner."

"Well, all right, so long as you apologize, I guess I'll forgive you. So where have you been anyway? I called your office, but that dingbat you have working for you told me her lips were sealed." He laughed.

"Who was that, Margaret or Candy?"

"The one with the funny voice."

"Margaret. She's just doing her job, Fred."

"Talking to her is a real trip. Why is it that private investigators always have secretaries with high voices?" He snorted with laughter.

I smiled with pride. Fred had unknowingly flattered me. He was talking like I was a real private investigator. "I don't know, but I've noticed that recently, too. So what's going on down there that I might want to know about?"

"No, you don't, Mavis. You bring me up to date first. You owe me that much."

"So I do, Fred. What would you say if I told you that someone just practically bashed in my head?"

"Just? Are you all right, girl?"

"Yeah, I'm okay. The cops wanted me to go to the hospital, but I'm sure this ice pack the EMTs gave me will do the job on my goose egg."

"You poor kid. Wait a minute. You said 'down there.' Where are you?"

"In Fort Worth."

"Fort Worth! What in the hell are you doing up there?"

"Investigating that murder. I told you I was on that."

"So tell, already. What's going on?"

"You have to promise to keep it to yourself until it's all over, okay?"

"Right. Let me get a pen."

"Ready?" I proceeded to give Fred the rundown on everything that I'd been able to find out about Doris Jones, including her real name. Between whistles and exclamations, we were on the phone for half an hour before I could get any information out of him.

"Well, that really blows the HPD theory, doesn't it?"

"I'd say so," I said smugly. I couldn't help it. After what I'd been through, I deserved it.

"So now you want the really big news?" he asked.

"Yeah, what else have you been able to find out?"

"There's been another strangulation down here."

"Really? That ought to keep them busy. Was it the same MO?"

"Yep. A stocking—but listen to this, Mavis. Your deceased was the only one killed with her own. The others were all the same brand and must have been brought in by the killer."

"Wow! When did they find the body?"

"Yesterday. They think that she wasn't supposed to be found until Memorial Day, a holiday, like the others, but the murderer didn't count on the landlady having the exterminator in to spray all the apartments. If he hadn't found her, she wouldn't have been missed for quite a while."

"I'm convinced that whoever killed Elizabeth was someone she knew, Fred. With everything I've heard, it couldn't have been the same killer—and she wouldn't have let anyone she didn't know inside her apartment. Carl told me so."

"I believe you. And someone up there wouldn't be ransacking your room and warning you off."

"Right. You know Ben Sorensen, Fred. Do you think if I told him everything now that he'd believe me? He didn't before."

"You two are on the outs, huh? I saw him the other day and asked about you. He was real short-tempered with me."

"He's angry. He didn't believe me, and he didn't want me to look into this. Same old story. But do you think I have enough to convince him now?"

Fred laughed. "Trying to find an excuse to call him?"

I sighed. "I guess so, but it would be nice to know he would know where I was in case something else happened. You know how it is."

"Are you worried, Mavis? Want me to come up there?"

"No, I don't want you to come up here, Fred. I don't even want Ben to come up here. I'm not a baby. I just thought you might give me a little fatherly advice."

"Thanks a lot. Kids I've got. Women I don't."

"C'mon, Fred. You know how I feel."

He sighed loudly. I knew it was all a tease. "Call him. The worst he could do would be to hang up on you, right?"

"Right. Okay. I'll let you know if I come up with anything else."

"Same here. Give me your number."

I did, and I gave him the name and address of the motel, and hung up. Then I gave HPD a ring, but Ben was out to dinner.

I was feeling nervous, very lonely and, I admit it, sorry for myself. My head ached like all get-out. I was hungry, but tired of evening meals alone. I was mystified as to whodunit. And for the life of me I couldn't figure out what anyone would want in my room. It was kind of creepy thinking that whoever it was might come back. I didn't want to be alone anymore. I didn't like the independence anymore. I decided to call The Rex.

After our initial greeting, I asked Carl whether he ever detected any sign of Doris being a drug user.

"Are you crazy, Mavis? If she'd used drugs, I would've known about it. What's going on up there, anyway?"

"I don't know, Carl. I'm getting more and more confused. The way I figure it, there are possibly three suspects: Vernon Spencer, her ex-law partner, is at the head of the list; following is her husband, who had a two-hundred-and-fifty-thousand-dollar life insurance policy on her; and lastly is a man named Willard Thompson, who is a known drug dealer and says she stole his drugs but that he didn't kill her."

"That's the craziest thing I ever heard. She didn't use 'em or I'd have known it. I've had druggie waitresses here before, and I can tell. And she couldn't have sold them. She didn't have enough opportunity except on her days off. I just refuse to believe it. Jesus!"

"I'm grasping at straws, Carl. I can't really find a motive for Spencer. It's just that he's strange and these other people I met think he did it. I don't really think Thompson did it, or why would he seek me out when I didn't even know he existed? That leaves Robert Reynolds, her husband, and according to their oldest daughter, she never told him where Elizabeth was. Not that he couldn't have found out some other way, I guess. I'm running in circles. I know I'm onto something. I just don't know what."

"Damn. Something's got to break. Did you hear about the other murder down here?"

"Yeah, I heard. I'm convinced Elizabeth Reynolds' death was not related, Carl. Other than the murderer being someone she knew, I just don't know who did it. Whoever that someone is thinks that I've got something they want."

"What?"

"Someone ransacked my room today and banged me on the head when I walked in on them, but I can't figure out what they think I have that they'd want."

"Jesus!"

"Would you stop saying that? Give me your ideas on this, Carl."

"Are you okay? Did you call the police? Maybe we'd better stop for your own good, Mavis. You want me to close up and come up there?"

"Yes, I'm okay. Just a little shaken up. And yes, I called the police, and no, don't come up here. Just help me figure out what they could think I have of Elizabeth's. That's got to be what they were looking for and her daughter told me that Elizabeth said she had some protection. I haven't a clue to what it was." But a thought just occurred to me. I suddenly remembered the large safe deposit box that contained nothing but rings.

"Beats the hell out of me, Mavis."

"Don't use that phrase, Carl. I hope that's not next on their list."

"Don't joke like that. You'll make me so worried that I'll regret having hired a woman."

"Oh, never that. I'm okay, and I'll continue to be okay. If they'd wanted to really hurt me, they already had their chance. Think about all this, Carl, and call me if you come up with anything, okay?"

"Sure thing, Mavis."

I hung up and went to dinner in the motel restaurant. The food lacked desirability, but I didn't have the wherewithal to drive. When I got back, I showered, took three aspirin, and got into bed. I was so tired that I didn't even consider the possibility that my visitor would return. I sank into a deep sleep.

I was dragged back to consciousness by a nagging sound that went on and on at regular intervals. I don't know how many times the phone must have rung before I finally reached for it.

"'Lo," I mumbled as I cradled the receiver and scooted down further under the covers.

"It's me, Willard," said the deep voice. "I've got some more information for you."

I was groggier than usual, probably because of the little incident earlier. It took a while before I realized who Willard was. I was snoozing off with the phone right up next to my ear.

"You listening? I said I got something to tell you," he said, the urgency in his voice dragging me out of my lethargic state.

"Um, go ahead," I muttered.

"I ain't comin' there. They're probably watching you. You got to come here."

"Can't. Can't drive tonight," I said sleepily.

"What's wrong with you? You awake?"

"Yup. Got hit. Can't drive tonight."

"Humph. Meet me tomorrow night then. Same place. Midnight." The phone clicked.

Chapter 25

WHEN I AWOKE EARLY THE NEXT morning, the receiver was on the floor and the noise coming from it was unbearable. It wasn't until I'd hung it up that I had a vague recollection of the call of the night before. What a dope I felt like.

I got dressed and headed back downtown. I was going to talk to that assistant district attorney if I had to wait around the courthouse all day. Carl was right; something had to break, and the only way it was going to was if I made it happen. Besides, I wanted him to know what had been going on in his jurisdiction as far as my bodily health was concerned.

I arrived outside the courthouse at the same time as Doyle Proctor. I saw him getting out of a new Corvette, so I followed him and soon introduced myself. He was wearing a blue pinstriped suit, the cloth of which appeared to be silk. The color brought out the blue of his eyes. His piercing, direct stare caught me off guard as it did the other day. I muttered my name to him and attempted to shake hands, but dropped my hand when he didn't take it.

There's a clue to a person's character in their handshake, I believe, and I'm automatically put off when someone won't take my hand. There's nothing wrong with my hand. I keep it clean, not smelly or sweaty. But the man refused it. He acknowledged me instead with a nod of his head.

"I'd like to talk to you if you have a few minutes, Mr. Proctor," I said as I followed him to the rather-steep stairs. I was looking around for an elevator, but he started climbing.

"In what regard, Miss Davis?" He was taking the steps two at a time, so I was forced to chase after him.

"Elizabeth Reynolds." I was huffing by the first landing. I really was going to have to consider quitting smoking.

He didn't flinch or turn around. He kept going. A constable passed us on the way up, as did a couple of men in suits who greeted Proctor and stared at me, but he still didn't stop. The district attorney's office had a glass door, a glass enclosure to the right, behind which a receptionist sat, and then another glass door. The reception area looked like a booth in a movie theater. I hoped I wasn't going to have to get a ticket to get inside. Proctor continued to walk ahead of me so I followed him, quickening my pace to keep up with him.

When we entered the office, he started back through the second glass door, ignoring me.

I didn't know whether to follow him or not. I was growing a little irate at his rudeness. I hollered at his back, "I want to talk about the way she set up her clients for y'all."

That got his attention. He pivoted around, his eyes searing through me, and stalked over to where I was standing. He grasped me roughly by the arm and said, "Come on back."

I did. And we went into his office where he seated me in a chair opposite his desk, closed the door, and sat across from me.

"Just what's this all about?" His expression matched his voice.

"Willard Thompson says that Elizabeth Reynolds set him up for a fall."

"Who's Willard Thompson?" He was leaning forward in his chair, his eyes unwavering and his lips pursed.

"He was a client of Elizabeth Reynolds at the time of her disappearance. You did the plea on him with Vernon Spencer after she'd gone."

153

He shook his head, apparently not remembering, and fingered the large gold ring on his right hand, twisting it.

"Let me back up a little, Mr. Proctor. You know Elizabeth Reynolds is dead, don't you?"

He leaned back in his chair, his eyes not leaving my face, and said, "Yeah. Spencer told me."

"Well, I've been hired to look into it."

"I know that, too."

I nodded, not surprised. It's been my experience that assistant DAs know a lot that they don't volunteer to the general public. "Anyway, I met with this Willard Thompson the other night. He's out on parole."

He nodded.

"He wanted to tell me that he didn't kill her. Then he told me that he suspected that she'd set him up because he was selling dope to the kids in her neighborhood. He acted like it was pretty-general knowledge in the jail that some lawyers do that."

"So?"

"So, I find that very hard to believe."

"The man's a criminal. What did you expect?"

"Did she set him up? Were you a party to that?"

"Listen, lady, do you know how many cases I handle in a year? Hundreds. I don't remember the names of the ones I did last month, much less last year." He laughed, but it wasn't congenial.

"You'd remember if Elizabeth set this guy up and then disappeared, wouldn't you? I mean, that's not an everyday occurrence around here—is it?" I stared back at him, forcing my eyes to be as unwavering as his.

"What exactly did this joker tell you? Where'd he get an idea like that, anyway?"

I sighed and shook my head at him. "I'm not sure how he thinks it came down, but he said he got arrested for holding, which I'm assuming means the same thing up here as it does in Harris County: that he was in possession of drugs. Then he said he called her from the jail. She had been his lawyer before. He wanted her to get him out. He was going to sell his dope when he got out and pay her to defend him. She refused to get him out. Then he said he told her that he'd tell her where the dope was, and she could sell it, and then get him out. He supposedly left her a message or something, and then she disappeared, so he thinks she stole his dope and left town. He claims he had enough so that she'd be able to live like a queen."

He was rolling his eyes and shaking his head. "This guy sounds like a real nut case, Miss Davis. You believed that?" He laughed again. This time there was a jovial ring to it.

"I don't know what to believe. I mean, why would he contact me to tell me a crazy story like that if it wasn't true?"

"Maybe he's covering up what really happened. Did you ever think of that?"

"I don't know. I'm just trying to find out who killed her, that's all. I don't care about any of that other stuff. It's not my business. I don't care if the lawyers in this town set up their mothers. I'm hired to find out who killed her and that's it. That's all I want to do. Then I want to go home where it's safe, where I know some people, where I can sleep in my own bed without being awakened in the middle of the night by weird phone calls, where people don't go around ransacking my room and hitting me over the head. That's all I want." I ended my monologue breathlessly. What I was doing crying on the shoulder of this cold fish, I'll never know.

"Sounds like you've been having a real good time," he said. I looked up into his face again, after wringing my hands, and his lips were tipped up into a little smile. Maybe he was human after all.

"It's been a real ball, let me tell you."

"You know, if all that has been happening, it sounds like someone is worried that you're on to something."

"But who? And what?"

"Maybe this Willard guy."

"I don't think so. If he was worried about me, he could easily have gotten rid of me the other night and no one would have known the difference."

"Yeah?"

"Yeah. We met some place in the boondocks and no one knew about

155

it, so he could have finished me off with no problem. He acts like he wants to help."

"Like I said, it could be a cover-up."

"I don't think so. He wants to meet again tonight, and I don't think he would do that if he was trying to hide something."

"Hmmm. What else have you got?"

"Besides him?"

He nodded again.

"A husband with a girlfriend and a two-hundred-and-fifty-thousand-dollar insurance policy. An ex-law partner that seems to be doing a much better business now that Elizabeth's gone." I watched his face for a reaction to either of my statements. He was good, very good. As an afterthought, I added, "A serial killer in Houston who the police down there want to pin it on." To that he showed mild surprise. "The Houston cops don't think she was killed by someone up here?"

Had I blown it? My mouth had overextended again. "I didn't have enough evidence to get them interested when I left there, but I tried to call one of them last night to bring him up to date. He was out to dinner."

"So they don't know about what's been happening up here? Hell, it doesn't matter. We're out of their jurisdiction anyway, but I wonder if they've contacted any of our men to touch base with them on it?"

"I don't think so. At least not yet."

"Tell you what, Miss Davis. How about if I put one of our investigators on this with you. I liked old Elizabeth. She was pretty cool, and I always wondered what had happened to her. You talk to Miguel, tell him everything you know, and maybe he can help you out. He's got his finger on the pulse of this town. If anyone can put this together, he can." He smiled and stood up.

I stood, also, and smiled back in surprise. I was flabbergasted by the offer. I half expected he'd throw me out of his office, and here he was offering help. Well, it was welcome. I was mystified and not a little scared.

"Where're you headed? You got time to talk to him now?"

I glanced at my watch. There was still time before lunch. "I was planning lunch with Elizabeth's former secretary, Tammy Bradley, but I have time to meet with him if he's here."

"Sure." He came from behind his desk and clapped me on the shoulder. "I'm glad you came in to see me. I was wondering who you were when I saw you in the courtroom the other day. I thought I knew everyone that hangs around the courthouse, but I knew I'd never seen that red hair before."

I laughed. "That's me. Unforgettable."

He opened the door and ushered me up more stairs to a smaller office. There he introduced me to Miguel Mirales. Better known as Mike. My first thought at seeing him was muscle-bound brat. He was short, stocky, young, and, from the looks of him in his shirt-sleeves, could pack a wallop.

The office had two small metal desks shoved up against each other at the wall. Papers were piled high upon each of them, the desk trays overflowing. Mike found me a chair from another office and brought it in so that I could sit in the two-foot aisle between the door and the farthest wall while we talked. He introduced me to the other investigator, who was on the phone. His name was Ray something-or-other, and he came and went while we spent the next hour or so holed up in there, with Mike taking my statement. At first Mike didn't seem much interested, but when the chief assistant tells you to do something, you do it. As I finished up my recitation, he indicated that he would do some checking and get back with me.

When I left the district attorney's office, I walked over to the Tandy Center once more, peeking in store windows, watching the ice skaters, and checking out the subway, passing the time until I had to meet Tammy. I even called Ben again, but he was still not there.

At the appointed hour, I arrived at the restaurant Tammy had suggested, and waited for her to meet me. And waited. And waited. Finally, thinking that she had chickened out, I called her office.

"Who's calling?" the female voice on the other end of the line asked me.

"Mavis Davis. We had a lunch date, but she never showed."

"Hold the line for Mr. Baldwin, please," the voice said.

Paranoia swept through me. What had I done wrong? Had the girl gone to her boss to get out of talking to me? All she had to do was decline. I mean, she would have had to decline in an aggressive way, I know I come on strong sometimes, but I would have taken no for an answer, eventually.

"Miss Davis?" an unfamiliar male voice asked.

"Yes," I replied with trepidation. I hate male authority figures.

"Miss Bradley can't meet with you today," his voice boomed.

"Oh, that's okay then." I didn't want a confrontation with an unknown. "Can I leave my number where she can get in touch with me so we can meet after hours?"

"No, Miss Davis. What I meant to say was that Miss Bradley can't meet with you at all. She's dead."

Chapter 26

AT HIS WORDS, A SHIVER STARTED at the back of my neck and scurried down my spine. The hair rose up on my arms. I couldn't respond.

"Miss Davis? Are you there?"

I nodded and tried to swallow the bubble in my throat. I was afraid to ask how it happened—afraid that I was responsible. I managed to utter the word, "When?"

"Just a few minutes ago—at lunchtime. She was on her way to meet you and got run over by a car. Hit-and-run."

My stomach turned over. Guilt consumed me like a thirsty drunk with a fresh bottle. "Did anyone see who was driving or get the license number?"

"The girl that was with her when she left the office is hysterical. In shock. We don't know whether she saw who it was or not. She came screaming into the office, and that's when some of the other people went out and found Tammy. The police are here now, Miss Davis. I'm sorry." He hung up.

What had I done? She had been safe for a year before I showed up. Now someone got scared and killed her. What could she have known? What had she said? I couldn't recall. Who had known I was meeting with Tammy Bradley? God. Only everybody.

I went back to the district attorney's office and waited for Mike Mirales. Would he be interested now? Or would he pass the buck to the police? I didn't know, but I wanted some reassurance from someone. What had I gotten myself into?

I heard some heavy footsteps and looked up to see Mirales come through the door with Doyle Proctor. They were laughing at something. When they saw me, they stopped dead in their tracks.

"Back already, Miss Davis?" Doyle Proctor asked, sounding annoyed.

I looked up at them from where I sat and thought that my mind must be going. Proctor stared at me with one eyebrow arched. Mike Mirales' look was a blank stare. I was suddenly suspicious of them, too. "Tammy Bradley was killed," I said, and to my humiliation, a tear ran down my face.

"Shit!" Mike said.

"Come on in the back," Proctor said, and helped me out of the chair.

I felt like a total fool as I wiped at my face with my fingers. It was my fault the girl died. Yet I was helpless to have stopped it. They led me to the library and put me in a chair at the conference table. Mike left and returned with some tissues that he pushed at me. I blew my nose while they sat opposite me and looked on. When I could breathe normally, they started at me with questions.

"How'd you find out about this?" Proctor asked.

"Remember I told you I was going to lunch with her?"

They both nodded.

"She didn't show up, so I called her office. I talked to a Mr. Baldwin, and he told me that on her way to meet me, she was run over by a car." I blew my nose again.

"Any witnesses?" Mike asked.

"I don't know. The girl that was walking with her had to be sedated, I guess. He said she was hysterical. He didn't tell me much. The police were there. He didn't say if anyone else saw what happened or not."

"I'll find out, Mavis, don't you worry," Mike said as he patted me on the arm.

I looked at him and back to Proctor. They really did seem sympathetic. I didn't know what else to say to them, so I just sat there for a few minutes.

Finally, Proctor said, "Why don't you go back to your motel and lie down for a while. I'm sure you'll feel better. Mike will call you if he turns up anything."

"I just feel so bad," I said.

"It's not your fault," Mike said.

Proctor just watched me. Accusingly, I thought.

"But if I'd never called her, she'd still be alive."

"You don't know that, Mavis," Mike said. "The killer might have had her on his list anyway."

"You just be careful that you aren't next," Proctor said.

Involuntarily, my body jerked at that statement. It was as if I'd been slapped. I looked at Proctor to see what he'd meant by it, but his face was deadpan. I turned to Mike. His face was drawn, his eyes watching me closely. The two of them made me nervous. I was now anxious to leave; ready to get the hell away from them. They walked me back out to the reception area, and Mike reassured me that he would call if he learned anything from the police.

When I reached my room, the red message light was lit on the phone again. I rang the motel office. They reported that a Benjamin Sorensen and a Margaret Applebaum had called. I immediately felt better. I didn't know how Ben had gotten the number, but I was glad. I returned the call. He wasn't in again. I was growing quite frustrated.

I called Margaret. Her voice made my throbbing head feel worse.

"Whatchadoin'?" she asked.

"I'm pulling off my clothes so I can take a nap." I had to smile in spite of myself. Some things always remained normal. "And returning your phone call, Margaret. How are you?"

"I'm fine. Candy's fine. Everything's fine. I finished the home study."

"You did? Already? That's great." I sat on the edge of the bed as I spoke to her. I wanted to get under the covers and pull them over my head. I wanted to stay there until this case was solved.

"Want me to read it to you? I wrote it up just like you did the others. I pulled an old one from a file and copied the format."

"Sure." It would be a relief to get my mind off Tammy Bradley for a few minutes.

Margaret started reading. She read our office name and address off the letterhead, the date, the cause number and style of the case. She read every last detail, even the sincerely yours and her name. That's Margaret. It was a comforting phone call.

After I hung up, I laid there for who knows how long trying to nap, but instead my mind wandered back to Elizabeth Reynolds and the pieces that wouldn't fit together. It was like trying to start a jigsaw puzzle with a corner piece missing.

I thought about all the characters I had met. Vernon Spencer always headed the list. Was that because the Newbolds suspected him? He'd seemed somewhat concerned about Elizabeth's death. What would he have had to gain? Was she hiding from him? If so, why? What could be so bad that she couldn't tell her husband? Had Spencer threatened her in some way? Why couldn't she have gone to the police? Did he know where she was? And if so, did he leave right after court, drive or fly down there, kill her, and then come back to continue his trial the next day?

Willard Thompson. He would have killed her if he'd had the chance. Did he indeed have the chance and was now covering up? Why would he have come forward like that? Why did he want to meet that night? How would he have known where she was?

Robert Reynolds should probably be at the head of the list. Many people would kill for money, and he would be the proud recipient of $250 thousand soon. Would he kill the mother of his children? He seemed to truly care for her. Did he do it out of love for Madge?

Who knew where Elizabeth was? And who would she have let into her apartment?

I couldn't help but get the feeling that something funny was going on in the district attorney's office. Doyle Proctor had answered very few of my questions. He never did admit that Elizabeth had set up some of her clients. He was a cold one. I didn't think that it was a necessary requirement that the chief assistant be that cold to someone who was trying to solve a crime. Maybe he hated private investigators. I certainly hadn't given him any reason to be as rude as he had been that morning.

My head went 'round and 'round, and finally I drifted off. When I awoke, it was to the ringing of the phone again. That was getting old.

I answered. It was Robert Reynolds. Would I come to dinner? They had some things they'd decided I ought to know.

My mind was whirling again. I got up, pulled on my shorts and shirt, and drove a couple of blocks to the laundromat. While my small supply of clothes was washing and drying, I got out my spiral notepad and reviewed the notes I had made from day one. Something was there, but I was missing what it was.

I moved through my notes rapidly. Couldn't grasp it. I felt like it was on the tip of my tongue or the edge of my consciousness. I wanted to open my brain and peer inside. If it was swimming around, I could reach in and grab it. I needed someone I could bounce ideas off. Even Margaret would do.

I assigned a page to each person I suspected, outlined what I knew about them and where they were when Elizabeth Reynolds was killed, and then it came to me. Just a little more investigation, and I could confirm who did it.

Chapter 27

WHEN MY LAUNDRY WAS DONE, I drove back to my room, careful to enter only after I'd made sure no one was there. Then I bathed, dressed, and arrived at the Reynolds' house sharply at 7:30 P.M.

"Hi," Catherine said glumly when she answered the door. She was dressed in white pants and layers of brightly colored blouses. Her face was solemn as she led me to the den where I saw that Anne and Mr. Reynolds were waiting for me literally on the edge of their chairs.

Mr. Reynolds jumped up. "Can I offer you a drink? I can fix almost anything," he said with a friendly smile. He was wearing one of those blazers with the college professor patches on the elbows.

"A Bloody Mary would be nice," I said as I perched on the edge of a bar stool at the portable bar in the back of the room. Funny, I'd never noticed it before. I glanced over my shoulder and saw Anne and Catherine huddled on the sofa together watching us.

The atmosphere in the room was stilted and awkward, much different from the previous visits. I wondered what was going on.

"You ever smoke dope, Mr. Reynolds?" I asked, and watched him while the vodka actually sloshed out of control when he reacted to my question. The girls were tittering behind me, but I ignored them and waited for Mr. Reynolds to recover himself so he could answer. Behind his glasses, his eyes had a stern, reprimanding look, and he cleared his throat.

"You really ought to call me Robert, Mavis. Especially if you're going to ask me intimate questions." He grinned suddenly. His face was rather nice like that.

"I thought it'd make a good ice breaker. Something's going on here, Robert. I can feel the tension in the air." I set my purse on the other black Naugahyde bar stool, sat back, and crossed my legs. I was hoping to give the impression that I wasn't leaving until I got some answers.

Slapping a napkin to the side of the glass, he handed me my drink and went on to mix himself a bourbon and Seven. "I'm a liquor man myself," he said as he poured. "Not that I didn't try marijuana once or twice when I was young; I did. We all did in the Sixties. But I didn't care for it. It seemed like it would be too easy to want to do it all the time, and I had a lot I wanted to do with my life." He stirred his drink and took a taste of it. "You girls want a Coke?" he called to the front of the room.

The girls came forward, as if on signal. "Yes, please," Anne said. She moved my purse up onto the bar and bounced up onto the stool beside me, looking at me closely and smiling. Catherine stood at my right. I was surrounded.

"Mavis was just inquiring as to whether I ever smoked dope, and I was telling her that I had experimented with it a couple of times when I was young. What do you girls have to say? Ever known me to do dope?"

"Nope," Anne said loudly, seeming to intentionally try to make it rhyme. "But you do drink alcohol too much, Daddy," she said and made a frowny face at him.

"Anne!" Catherine said.

"Well, he does. I wish you wouldn't drink at all, Daddy."

Robert handed them their soft drinks and didn't reply.

"I've never known Father to do any type of narcotics, Mavis," Catherine said with a frown at her sister. "And I think I would have been able to tell. We had an assembly at school once where the police came and told us all about drugs and how to tell if someone was doing them. You know, bloodshot eyes and funny behavior. And Father really only has a few drinks every night. It's not that much."

"I wasn't trying to start a family feud," I said as I looked from Catherine to Anne. "I'm just trying to put this thing together. Sometimes tactless questions are the only way I know of to go about it. What about Elizabeth, Robert? Did she ever use drugs?"

"Lord, no. She hated them. That's one of the things she was fighting over there in her old neighborhood. If it was up to her, she'd lock the drug dealers up and throw away the key," he said.

"Mother used to question me about the kids at school, Mavis," Catherine said. "She was always afraid that I'd get in with the wrong crowd. She wanted to know if I knew if drugs were available on campus, who was doing them, and stuff like that."

"Mom drank too much, too," Anne said.

My head was bobbing from side to side as I watched and listened to each of them. My head involuntarily jerked over toward Anne now as she surprised me with that statement.

"How can you say that, Anne?" Robert glared at his daughter.

Anne crossed her arms defensively in front of her. "Well, she did. Sometimes when she'd come home after I'd gone to bed, she'd come into my room to kiss me goodnight and I'd smell it on her breath." She ducked her head and watched her father with brooding eyes.

Robert sighed and came from behind the bar to where his youngest daughter was sitting. He put his arms around her and pulled her head against his chest. He stroked her hair. "I don't want that to be how you remember your mother though, Anne. She didn't do that a lot, and it wasn't until the last year that she did it at all." He looked over at me, his eyes sad. "She did start drinking more in the months not long before she left, Mavis. She'd do it before she came home. I don't know whether it was at the office or if she'd go out somewhere, but when she'd come home it was often quite evident that she'd had a little too much."

"Did you ever ask her for an explanation?" I asked.

"Not at first. I thought she must be going to happy hour with friends or something, but later, when it got to be more frequent, I did. She was real close-mouthed about it, saying that work was just getting to her."

"But she never used drugs as far as you know?"

"Absolutely not. Why do you keep harping on that?" he asked harshly. "I told you how she felt about them." He released Anne and stood staring at me, his arm dangling across the back of her bar stool.

I sipped my drink, pondering whether he had a need to know about the cache of drugs Thompson talked about. What the heck, all he could do would be give me an honest reaction. "A former client of hers told me that she stole his dope while he was in jail."

"That's absurd! Elizabeth would never do that. I'm surprised that she'd even represent the man."

"Mother really didn't like dopers, Mavis," Catherine said. "She hated them."

I looked at Catherine leaning up against the side of the bar reaching for the Coke can to refill her glass. She'd been straight with me so far. I didn't think she'd lie now.

"Believe me, I'm just trying to make sense out of everything I've been told. The man insists that he told her where he'd hidden some drugs, and that he'd asked her to get it out of hiding and sell it and get him out of jail, but she disappeared after that and so did his dope."

"You're kidding!" Robert said. "That's just not Elizabeth!"

"Okay, then tell me, would Spencer?"

"No." Robert's eyes lowered. A troubled expression came over his face. He walked back around the bar and picked up his drink, taking a long swallow. He set it down and looked me in the eye. "To tell you the truth, Mavis, I don't know if he would or not."

"That's what I thought."

"What do you mean by that?"

"I mean it seems awfully curious to me that he seems to be doing so well."

"I know."

"Have you seen his office?"

"Yes." He swirled the ice around in his highball glass and took another swig of his drink. "I went over there a couple of times to pick up checks from him. It's nice."

"It's more than that, Robert," I said. "It's plush."

"He could have gotten some real good personal injury suits though, Mavis."

"He would have had to settle them for an awful lot of money in the last year."

He shook his head. "I'd hate to think Vern would do that."

I swallowed the dregs of my Bloody Mary and put the glass down. "Well, it seems someone is setting up people to be busted and possibly selling the drugs somewhere in the process. Or maybe the other way around.

"I just don't know," Robert said.

"Let's go in to dinner," Catherine said softly. I glanced at her. She seemed downcast. My guess was that she had her own ideas about people and was disappointed at what I suspected.

I slipped off the edge of my stool and picked up my purse. Catherine and Robert led the way out of the room. Anne and I followed.

Anne pulled on my hand as we walked. "Mavis?"

"Yes?" I looked down at her.

"I always liked Vernon. He was nice to me." Her eyes were clouded over, and her face was drawn up in a frown.

I slipped my arm around her shoulders. "I know."

"He used to play with me when I was little. Sometimes, when school was out, Mama would take me to the courthouse with her, and Vernon would be there. He'd hug me and tease me, and people would look at us funny, but I didn't care. I knew it was because he was black—but I didn't care." Her eyes were searching my face.

I stopped and looked her dead in the eye. "Listen, Anne, if Vernon Spencer did something wrong, it had nothing to do with you, and it had nothing to do with his being black. I want you to remember that, okay?"

She nodded. "We don't know for sure that he did do anything to my mother."

"No. We don't. If I find out, I'll let you know."

"Okay."

We started walking again, and I caught Catherine looking back at us. A melancholy smile tugged at the corners of her mouth.

The dining room was rather small. It was off to the side of the kitchen. We sat in matching cushioned chairs at a long, dark wood table. The only other furniture in the room was a china cabinet. The walls were covered with beige-and-pink-striped wallpaper.

Catherine brought out a roast that she boasted she'd made herself, and we had potatoes, gravy, Brussels sprouts, and carrots. We talked of other things while we ate. There were a lot of long silences when I supposed everyone was thinking about either what had been said or what was to come. I still didn't know why I'd been asked to dinner.

When we were through eating, Catherine brought out coffee. I didn't have the heart to tell her that I was a tea sipper so I loaded up my cup with milk and sugar and tried not to grimace too much with each swallow.

"You're a great cook, Catherine," I said when she sat back down after clearing the plates away.

She smiled brightly and said, "And I'll make someone a good wife someday, right?"

I laughed. "I wasn't going to say that. I would never say something like that."

She grinned. "Good. Dad would."

Robert smiled at his eldest daughter. "Can I help it if I'm old-fashioned and want my daughter to have a good marriage?"

"Don't start." Catherine warned her father with a smile.

"Her mother was a good cook, too, Mavis. At least she was in the early days. She wasn't home later to do it, but I always helped out anyway, so it worked out okay."

"Yeah," Anne chimed in. "Daddy makes great spaghetti. Madge always gets onto him to make something besides spaghetti and hamburgers."

I watched their faces to get a reaction to my next words. "I understand that Madge spends quite a lot of time around here. Where is she tonight? I was hoping to see her."

"She wasn't invited," Catherine said coldly.

"Oh?"

"Catherine and Madge don't always see eye-to-eye, Mavis," Robert said.

"She's always butting into our business," Anne said. "It's okay most of the time, but sometimes she gets on Catherine's nerves."

I laughed. "Who told you that?"

"Catherine. She gets on mine, too, but I don't let it get to me. You see, Mavis," Anne said with a cocky look at her father, "Catherine and I figure that Madge likes Dad, but we're not sure how we feel about that."

"Anne!" Robert said sharply.

She glanced at me, then at Catherine, and back at her father. "Well, we're not. You said you weren't either. I heard you talking to her the other day."

"Were you eavesdropping on my conversation, young lady?"

"Just a little bit. I wish I'd heard the whole thing," she said to her father. She turned to me, "See, Mavis, I didn't know this, but Catherine knew where Mom was and was writing to her. They didn't tell me that until today. I made them tell me when I heard them talking. It explained what I'd heard before. Catherine had told Dad, but not me." Her eyes cut over to Catherine and her father, and she was frowning at them.

"Is that true, Robert?"

He sighed. "Pour me some more coffee, Catherine," he said and then looked at me. "Yes and no. Catherine was writing to her, but didn't know where she was."

"She knows all that, Dad. I told her the other day," Catherine said.

I nearly fell out of my chair. The dynamics of the conversation, not to mention the whole situation, were getting interesting.

"Mavis and I had a long talk after school," she said as she poured the coffee.

"You did? Why wasn't I informed?"

"I didn't know—I wasn't sure if I could trust you, Dad." Catherine's face was a study. Her expression was open and honest.

"Thanks a lot," he said dourly.

"Well, I didn't. You've been so upset and I thought Mavis needed to know some things"

"But you didn't tell me you'd told your father, Catherine," I said.

"You mean that I was writing to her in Dickinson?"

"Yes."

"I wasn't sure I wanted to do that, Mavis. I'm sorry. I was afraid that Father was somehow involved. I wanted to talk it out with him, which is exactly what we've done."

"So you knew all the time that your wife was at least receiving letters in Dickinson, Mr. Reynolds?"

"No, not all the time. Hey, don't go formal on me, Mavis, please. I didn't kill my wife."

"Sorry, slip of the tongue."

"Freud."

"Right. I guess everyone is a suspect."

"Catherine just told me a few weeks ago. She wanted me to try and find Elizabeth again and get her to come back. Madge wanted me to divorce Liz and marry her and Catherine was trying to stop it."

"Did you go and find her?" I asked.

He sighed and clutched at his napkin. "God, I wish I had." The room grew still.

"I was afraid she didn't want me, Mavis."

The girls were watching their father. He suddenly looked like an old man. Catherine reached over from beside him and put her hand on his. Anne looked at me and then pushed her chair back and went over and hugged him around the neck.

"And what did Madge think of all this?"

"She's always known how I felt about Elizabeth."

"Did she want you to go find her and see how Elizabeth felt about you?"

"Yes, but I just couldn't do it. I was afraid, I guess."

"What did Spencer think? Did you tell him?"

"He thought I should leave well enough alone."

"Where were you on Monday night of last week?"

"He was here, Mavis," Catherine said. She held up her palm. "I swear. He was grading exams."

Chapter 28

SO THERE I AM, DRIVING BACK to my motel thinking that these things aren't so easy. I'm also thinking that it's a shame poor Elizabeth didn't know that her daughter let the cat out of the bag.

I parked the car and was crossing the parking lot to my room when out of nowhere the elusive hit-and-run driver came toward my body, no lights on, doing ninety to nothing. If I'd had my wits about me, he, or she, wouldn't have had a chance. It wouldn't even have been a close call, except that I was thinking about Elizabeth and all the people that could have found her, and wondering who did.

There were no screeching tires like on television, no bright lights glaring a warning at me, and if it hadn't been for my keen sense of hearing—my mother always said I had big ears—I would have worms crawling in and out between my toes right now.

Unfortunately, as I dove out of the way onto the pavement between two parked cars, I didn't stop to look at the driver. I couldn't say if there even was one. The police kept asking me over and over—before they sent me off in an ambulance to get my bumps and cuts checked—what color the car was, its make and model, and I couldn't remember that either. Some detective. I think rule six or seven is something about an investigator being observant. Great. I'm establishing quite a reputation for myself.

After the attendants in the emergency room checked me over and put bandages on my face, knees, and elbows, and after I refused to spend the night in the hospital, I caught a cab back to my motel.

It was almost straight-up twelve o'clock, and I was supposed to meet the midnight rider, Willard Thompson, in downtown Fort Worth. Without stopping in my room to freshen up, I carefully transferred from the cab to my car. I looked both ways before coming out into the open. Trust me, Mother.

I was late, and I knew it, but I hoped that Willard was a patient person and wouldn't abandon hope. My eyes were glued to the rearview mirror. I wasn't taking any chances. No one was there, and I finally made it to the appointed corner at about twenty-five after.

The bright lights flashed on and off and on again. When the car did a U-turn and sped off down the road, I followed. He went hither and yon again until I was totally lost. Finally he stopped at the side of the road in another sleazy section with which I was unfamiliar.

There were dark ramshackle houses spaced widely apart on the opposite side of the street. On our side were a couple of rickety old buildings that looked like they had been condemned. To say that the area was not well lit would be a gross exaggeration. If it hadn't been for the half-moon shining from up above, I wouldn't have been able to see my hand in front of my face.

He got out and approached my car. I could see by my headlights that it was indeed Willard, much to my relief. I had no way of knowing until then. I wasn't hesitant to talk with him this time. My curiosity got the better of me and, after cutting my lights, I hopped out, anxious to hear what he had to tell me.

"Hi, Mr. Thompson," I said to the tall, dark figure that loomed over me. I moved toward the hood to sit upon it. My knees ached when I stood too long. I perched on the side of the car feeling the warmth from the engine. There was no breeze. I could hear the crickets chirping somewhere in the darkness.

He squinted at me. "What happened? You been in a fight or something?"

"Or something. Someone tried to run over me, but they missed."

"Goddamn!"

"My sentiments exactly."

"I knew this thing was big! Listen, Miz Davis, you're in more trouble than ya know. You and I dug up more than we should've, and your asking questions got a lot of shit stirrin'." He stood too close to me in the dark and was whispering fiercely even though there was nobody else around.

"What are you talking about?" I asked, leaning away from him, trying to get a clear picture of his expression.

Headlights were coming slowly down the road, and Thompson was keeping his face toward them, watching. I started watching, too.

Without looking at me, he said, "I found out that there's some big people involved in the drug business in this town, and I don't want no part of it."

The car inched closer and finally passed us, moving slowly in the opposite direction. It was a small, dark, four-door sedan, its tinted windows bordering illegality. Thompson shifted his attention to me. "Ya get my drift?"

"No. What people? Are you sure this is something I need to hear? Otherwise—don't tell me. I don't want to know." I found myself whispering also, but wondering why.

"Big people. People in control."

"Who, for Christ's sake? I don't want to play games with you. If you know who, tell me."

He looked behind himself, and all around, as if there might be someone close by to listen to what he said. He started whispering again, "Cops, and defense lawyers, and—"

Suddenly a set of lights came at us. Startled, I hopped off the hood of the car. The approaching lights weren't a hundred feet away.

"Get down!" he yelled at me and I ran as best I could between my car and his. He was following after me when the first shots rang out. "Oh shit!"

I duck-walked, if you can call it that, around to the back side of my Mustang, and Mr. Thompson wasn't far behind me as the car passed by.

I heard the screeching of tires that I hadn't heard earlier in the evening and peeked up over my car to see what looked like the same dark-colored sedan doing a U-turn.

"Run, Mr. Thompson! Behind that building!" I called out to him as I hobbled as fast as I could from the roadside. I stumbled into the drainage ditch that was concealed by tall weeds, struggled through it, and ran toward the back of the dilapidated building that was closest to my car.

I heard more gunshots from the street as I reached my destination. The thought occurred to me that I might buy a gun if I ever got out of this situation. I didn't hear Mr. Thompson behind me, and I crouched down and came from around the back of the building in time to see the car do another turn. Mr. Thompson's dark shape was crawling in my direction. He was so big that if they were looking while they turned their car around they would easily be able to make him out.

I ran to help him, grabbing at one of his huge arms as I reached him. "Get down, dummy!" he said fiercely.

I dropped to the ground as the next round of shots began. "Are you okay?" I asked.

"No. I been hit. Keep down!"

We both began crawling as fast as we could. When we reached the back of the building, Mr. Thompson just sank to the ground. I waited, and yes, even prayed a little. I was expecting whoever it was to come after us on foot. I listened for footsteps in the brush, my breathing too loud in my ears. My heart was pounding like a bass drum.

"Mr. Thompson, do you have a gun?" I whispered.

He didn't answer me. I reached out in the darkness to feel for his hands. He had rolled over. One hand was clutching his side, and the other a long, dark object. My hands met with a warm, sticky substance when I touched his arm. I got closer, reaching for the dark object. It was some kind of a revolver. I unwrapped his fingers from around it, and took hold of the handle. If it was blood that I'd felt, it was all over the gun, too.

Pointing it away from the two of us, I found the release and flipped the cylinder open. I couldn't see well, so I picked each shell out until I determined that there were still two bullets left. Snapping it shut, I made sure the bullets were next to the chamber, ready to fire. Then I leaned up against the building and waited for them to come and get us, my finger on the trigger. The little that I know about guns, Ben taught me, but I'm not afraid of learning more. Necessity is the mother of invention and all that.

And that's how the authorities found us. I heard their sirens from far off, but I wasn't about to move. Who knew how crazy the shooters were. Besides, somewhere in the back of my brain, I'd thought I'd heard Mr. Thompson say something about cops and defense lawyers.

The sirens grew closer and closer until they stopped. I could see the flash of lights. I kept my position until I heard footsteps in the brush and saw the beam from flashlights, then I called out to them. "There's two of us here. The man with me has been shot and needs medical attention. When you come around the comer of the building, I want to see some identification because I'm armed and scared."

I could hear some static from a radio, and then, "TarrantCounty Sheriff's Department, ma'am. Put down your gun. We aren't going to hurt you."

"I want to see some ID. Please!"

A few seconds later, something solid landed near my feet. I felt around on the ground until I found it. It was a shield pinned to a leather holder. I could feel the raised numbers.

"Okay, deputy. Come on."

"Throw out your weapon, ma'am."

I began an "Our Father," and tossed the revolver toward the side of the building. Seconds later, a beam of light struck me in the eyes. I could barely make out a dark shadowy form behind it, and then another. The men approached us warily, their guns drawn. I stayed where I was. If these were crooked cops, and I was dead meat, there was nothing I could do but finish my prayer.

The flashlight was lowered, and I was given a hand up. I dusted myself off as I asked the deputy for an ambulance.

"Already got one on the way. You all right?"

"Yeah. A little scared, maybe, but, yeah, I'm fine."

The second man was bending over Willard. "He's hit pretty bad, but still breathing," he said as he shined the light over his body. "Caught it in the side."

"Poor Willard," I said, as I leaned over him. His breathing was raggedy.

"What in the hell's been going on here, ma'am?" asked the first officer.

I could hear another siren as we waited in the dark for the ambulance. "Could I have a minute with my friend?" I needed to talk to Willard before they took him away. As soon as the second deputy stood up to talk to his partner, I crouched down over Willard. "Mr. Thompson, can you hear me?" I asked in a soft voice. I could see his eyes open a little crack and he nodded slightly. "I have to ask you, what were you going to tell me?" I had a theory about why Elizabeth disappeared. I needed Willard's confirmation. He mumbled something, but I couldn't understand him. I put my hands on his cheeks and looked down into his face. "Nod if you can understand me," I said. I could feel him nodding slightly.

"They're coming with a stretcher, ma'am," said one of the officers.

I whispered in Willard's ear. "Nod, Willard, if you were going to tell me that there are Fort Worth cops and defense lawyers involved in dealing dope."

He nodded and then whispered something again. It sounded like district attorney. My heart skipped a beat.

"DAs? Nod if it's DAs, Willard," I whispered.

His head bobbed up and down.

Chapter 29

WILLARD'S EYES OPENED WIDE WITH WHAT I can only assume was fear, since that's what was clutching at my stomach. I smiled at him and patted his cheek. "You're a good man, Willard, and a good friend. You rest now, and I'll see what I can do about taking care of the situation."

I could hear more footsteps in the long grass. As I stood up a pair of uniforms with a stretcher came 'round the corner at us. They fetched Willard and took him away.

The two deputies and I followed the stretcher out to the street where there were three sheriff's cars parked helter-skelter—bubble lights flashing—and more deputies examining our cars. As we reached the ditch, I could hear one man say, "Shotgun, here."

Another said, "Looks like a large-caliber handgun over here."

The street was littered with glass. The driver's side of my Mustang was full of holes, my windows and tires blown out. I felt a terrific urge to blubber like a baby.

They wanted to deluge me with questions. I wanted to check my car out. I went over to pop the hood open.

"What are you doing, lady? You can't touch that. It's evidence," a deputy said. He'd come over and put his big hand on the hood.

"I just want to see if I'll be able to drive it if I get the tires fixed."

"Somebody tried to kill you tonight and you're worried about whether you can drive your car? Hey, Lou," he called to another deputy, "did the paramedics check this lady out? I think she's in shock or something."

"Lady, are you sure you're all right?" It was the first deputy. The one who'd come out behind the building and found us. "Even if you could drive your car, you're going to have to answer some questions before you can go anywhere."

"I just want to look under the hood," I said, reaching for the hood again.

I could tell they thought I was nuts, but I had to know. It was easier than concentrating on what Willard had told me. I needed time to mull that over in my mind. And I needed time to decide whom I could trust.

"Okay, go ahead, but I don't know what you can tell in the dark."

I popped the hood and raised it and stood staring at the engine, feeling like a dummy. They were right, and I knew it, but fear was preventing me from thinking clearly. What was I doing in a strange town where I didn't know anyone, where I didn't know who I could trust, where I didn't even know if I'd be able to get home?

The deputy who the other had called Lou shined his flashlight around the engine for me. "Satisfied?" he asked.

"Start it for me?"

He went around and got in and started my car. Then he shut it off, got out, and brought my purse and keys to me. I slammed the hood.

"Ready to make a statement now?" Lou asked.

I opened my purse, dropped my keys inside, and studied the interior, looking for an answer. How did I know he wasn't in on the whole thing?

"You want to come sit inside my car where we can talk?"

I nodded and let him lead me to his car, which was sticking halfway into the street, door hanging open, lights still flashing. After we got in, he cut off the lights and pulled over to the side of the road. He turned off the engine and turned on the inside lights. He was young, in his upper twenties, but had gray in his light-brown hair. His face was lined with fatigue. He had brown eyes and a mustache, and wore the short-sleeved khaki uniform of the sheriff's department.

"Your name is Mavis Davis, right?"

"How'd you know?"

"One of the other men checked your identification in your purse and ran a license plate check. Sorry, but we didn't know what we'd find when we pulled up."

"It's okay."

"The man with you. What's his name?"

"Willard Thompson, and that's all I know about him except he's on parole. I don't know where he lives or anything."

"Mind telling me, Miss Davis, what you were doing out here in the middle of the night with someone like Thompson?"

I sighed. I might as well tell him as much of the truth as possible. "He was giving me evidence to use in a murder investigation." I watched for his reaction and was rewarded when his attention quickly shifted from his notepad to me.

"You're not a police officer."

"Private."

"Where's your ID?"

"It's here." I dug around in my purse until I came up with my card case, which I showed to him. Then I dug around some more and found my cigarettes. I was trying to light up, but my hands were shaking so badly that the deputy took my lighter away and held it for me. Any thoughts of quitting had been shoved to the back of my mind.

"Sure you're okay?" He frowned at me.

I blew smoke away from him. He was trying to be nice. "Yeah."

"So why are you really up here?"

"On a murder, I told you. The chief assistant DA knows about it. Doyle Proctor?"

"Since when?" He was a disbelieving so-and-so.

"Today? Yesterday? I'm confused, what day is it?"

He didn't answer me. "You talked to him about it?"

"Yes, and to Miguel Mirales who Proctor assigned to it."

"So what's the victim's name?"

"Victims. Plural. At first, it was just Elizabeth Reynolds. Now you can add Tammy Bradley and maybe Willard Thompson—if he dies."

"Elizabeth Reynolds the lawyer?"

"Yes. Did you know her?"

"She used to come to the jail when I was assigned there. She disappeared a couple of years ago."

"Last year. Somebody killed her in Houston. That's where I'm from."

"Humph."

"What's that supposed to mean?"

"Sounds like a fishy story."

"It's the truth. Call Mirales. Call Proctor."

"I will, or my supervisor will, tomorrow." He stared at me with apparent skepticism.

"I'm telling you the truth. Honest."

"So who was trying to kill you? Who was in that car?"

"I have my suspicions," but I wasn't going to tell him. "I don't have any proof. It might not even be related. For all I know, it could be someone out to get Mr. Thompson and have nothing whatever to do with me." I was blowing smoke.

"Why would someone want to kill Thompson?"

"How would I know? I never met the man before a few nights ago."

"What was he on parole for?"

"Drugs."

"Shit, lady! You're in a lot of trouble then. You better start talking while you've got the chance."

It's unnecessary to say that fear clutched at my stomach again. "Why do you say that?"

"Got some serious problems with druggies in this town."

"What town doesn't?"

"You don't understand. I heard that—" he suddenly realized who he was talking to, I guess, because he stopped and looked at me again, suspicion peeping out from under his eyelids. "If you know something, you'd better spill it, that's all."

"Not to you. I want a grand jury."

"What?" His voice went up a pitch.

"I'm not talking to anybody but a grand jury. You heard me."

"Are you nuts?"

"No, and I'm not talking anymore. Can someone drop me back at my motel? I need a bath, and I'm awfully tired."

"I could arrest you. Take you into custody."

"For what?"

"Discharging a firearm in a public place."

"Go ahead."

"Come on, lady. Just cooperate."

"Arrest me or take me to my motel."

"Shit!" he said, and yanked on the handle of his door. He got out, slamming the door behind him.

I watched as he went back and conferred with the others. After a few minutes, Lou returned to the car in the company of another deputy.

"We're taking you to your motel," he said disgustedly. "Get in the back seat."

"What about my car?" I asked as I got out and then back in again.

"It'll be towed to the county lot."

"Somebody going to change my rear tire first?"

"Somebody will change your rear tire first," he said tiredly. "You can pick it up when the investigation is over."

"Great," I said, hoping he'd hear the sarcasm in my voice.

"Cooperate, Miss, and we'll see if we can't get it back for you sooner," the other deputy said over the back of the seat.

"I said I'd cooperate. I'll talk to a grand jury."

"Why won't you talk to us?"

"It's inadvisable, that's all."

"What about the DA?"

"Proctor? No."

"No, I mean the real district attorney."

"I dunno." I was tired. I couldn't think. How did I know whom I could trust? "Can't I decide tomorrow?"

"So long as you don't leave town."

"I thought cops weren't supposed to tell people that unless they were suspects."

"Wrong. We're not supposed to tell people to *leave* town."

"Oh."

"We're only going to take you back if you promise to come to the district attorney's office tomorrow morning. We'll send a car to pick you up."

"Okay, I promise, but I can tell you that I'm not talking to anyone except a grand jury."

"We heard you already," Lou muttered under his breath. The rest of the trip they were silent. So was I. We arrived at my motel at about two-thirty.

"You going to be okay?" Lou asked as I opened the car door. The anger that had been on his face earlier was replaced with a look of concern.

"Yeah. I'm going to barricade myself inside and get some sleep. Thanks for the ride. Sorry I gave y'all a hard time." I smiled and shrugged at them as I shut the door.

They waited while I got my key in the lock and opened the door, and I waved at them as they drove off. I closed the door behind me and pulled a chair up and put it under the knob. I went over and dropped my purse on the dresser. Then I heard someone clear his throat. My heart went pitter-patter and flitting through my brain was the wish that I'd kept Willard's gun. Then I turned around slowly to see who was there. It was Ben, big as life, standing in the doorway to the bathroom.

"I thought you said you were going to Austin to visit a friend," he said.

Chapter 30

THREW MYSELF ON HIM. HONEST TO God, I was so glad to see Ben, that I forgot my pain, ran to him, and threw myself on him. He wrapped his big arms around me, and we stood there until I was almost feeling secure again. Then he released me.

"You look like hell, Mavie," he said as he led me over to the bed where we both sat down. "What's going on? Someone been beating on you?"

I didn't want to talk. I wanted to be held, to feel safe, to curl up next to him and go to sleep, drift off into unconsciousness. But he wasn't going to let me do that, and I knew in my heart that I had things I was going to have to take care of in the morning with which he would be able to help.

I tugged off my shoes and sprawled out on the bed, leaning against the headboard, facing Ben. Now was the time to spill my guts, as Carl would say. Ben was the reinforcements, arriving in the nick of time. I told him the story from beginning to end, leaving out only the parts that weren't really relevant but which might only serve to get me into unneeded trouble.

He listened attentively, making appropriate facial expressions when I mentioned the parts about the physical abuse to my body, and didn't interrupt me unless I didn't explain myself well.

When I was through, when I had told him who I thought was responsible, we discussed a game plan. With his help and his contacts, it would all be over the following day. I set my travel alarm for seven o'clock. My first priority was Elizabeth's murder, and there was somebody I had to call to meet me for breakfast.

Then I took a hot bath, curled up in Ben's arms, and went to sleep.

The next morning I made a phone call that confirmed my suspicions. Next, I phoned the sheriff's department to tell them I had a ride to the courthouse. Then I made my breakfast-date call. We agreed to meet in the Tandy tunnel at nine o'clock. I had extracted a promise from Ben to do things my way, so he phoned some honest cops he knew for backup, and drove me downtown.

Before approaching the table at the Japanese Beef or Chicken Bowl, where we had agreed to meet, I went through the serving line for tea and a doughnut. And courage. Then I approached the murderer.

"Good morning," I said.

"Good morning."

"Sorry I had to meet you like this on such short notice, but I have to be in the district attorney's office in a little while."

"That's all right. What can I do for you?"

"Give yourself up."

"What?"

I narrowed my eyes like Ben does when he's angry. "May I see your key ring?"

"My key ring?" Her eyebrows drew together. "Sure." She pulled the string of keys from her purse and handed them to me.

I glanced down at her keys. The one I was looking for wasn't there. "What'd you do with the safe deposit box key, Madge? Throw it away after you removed the evidence against Spencer?"

"I don't know what you're talking about," she said defiantly.

"Yes you do. You're the only one who would know what I was talking about. You removed whatever it was that Elizabeth had taken to protect herself and her family against Vernon Spencer."

"Oh yeah?"

"Yeah. It's probably hidden in your house, Madge. Some papers or files or something." I hadn't expected to get a confession out of her. I don't know what I expected. She just sat there, staring at me with a deadpan look on her face.

"When you found out recently that Catherine had been writing to Elizabeth, and where, you staked out the post office until you finally saw her go to see if she had a letter from Catherine. Then you followed her bus home. She let you inside in spite of the fact that she was surprised to see you. You went up the back stairs. That's why Carl, the owner of The Rex Cafe, didn't see you."

"You're crazy, Mavis."

"You probably told her some lame excuse for coming to see her, and she didn't want Carl Singleton to know anything out of the ordinary was going on, so she went down and had dinner with him. Right?"

"I haven't seen Elizabeth in a year. I don't know why you think I could be involved in such a thing."

"Because of the baby, Madge. I'll lay you odds that you can't have any more children."

Her complexion paled. The skin on her face grew tight, like it was stretched back to her ears.

"Did you tell her that she couldn't go home again because you had her protection, her proof that Spencer, and whoever it is in the district attorney's office, are involved in drug trafficking? Did you ask her if she had made a copy of the files or whatever it was?"

"No, because I don't know anything about any files."

"Well, if she did, you got them," I said, answering my own question. "You told her that you wanted her to divorce Robert and never come back to the Fort Worth area, right? Or else you'd tell Spencer where she was and that she no longer had any evidence against him. She didn't know Catherine had told Robert. And Robert, being a trusting soul, had told you and probably Spencer. Am I not correct, so far?"

"You're being ridiculous. Why would I do such a thing?"

"Because you want Robert, Madge, that's why. He had a ready-made family for you. You told me yourself that you were more of a mother to those girls than Elizabeth was."

"Don't be stupid!"

I took a sip of my tea as I watched her angry face. "Maybe you killed her because you'd found out that Robert had her life insured for two-hundred-and-fifty-thousand-dollars and you wanted a part of the good life."

"That's absurd. I don't care anything about money."

"Right. Why would you when you'd been blackmailing Spencer."

"Blackmailing Spencer! Me? Wha—"

"Let's not play games, Madge. I know all about the blackmail bit. But, that wasn't your motive for killing Elizabeth. Maybe you really thought you loved Robert and it had to do with his telling you that he could never marry as long as he knew Elizabeth was alive. Or maybe she simply refused to divorce him."

Madge sat there before me, her arms crossed. The expression on her face was not getting any friendlier, I must say.

"I'm not real clear what your reasons were, Madge, but I figure it this way: Elizabeth told you she was supposed to eat dinner with Carl, so you saved the heavy-duty stuff until she came back. Then, for some insane reason, you killed her. You got a pair of stockings from her lingerie drawer and strangled her. You're strong; you work out; you could do it."

Madge's eyes cast about, as if seeking out the exits, and then came to rest upon mine. "How did you know?"

"Several things, but mostly the cruise." I was trying not to sound as smug as I felt, but it was hard.

"The cruise?"

"Yep. You're the only one with the opportunity. You shouldn't have told me that you'd stayed a day in each port. Robert told me it was a two-week vacation. And I called a travel agent who explained the workings of a cruise to me."

"Damn!"

"And I knew that Elizabeth wouldn't have let just anyone into her apartment. Carl said she was real secretive and careful, so it had to be someone she knew. She would have freaked if Spencer appeared at the door. Besides, he was in trial and didn't have the time to stake out the post office. It had to be Robert or you. And then there was the key. Carl had seen two safe deposit box keys, but later only one turned up. I knew she must have sent the other one to someone she trusted. Sort of back-up protection. Right? If she couldn't find help before she was found, you'd have the evidence to take to the authorities."

"You think you're so smart. Why didn't she give the key to Robert?"

"Robert wouldn't have had any part of it. He would have insisted she stay home. She couldn't tell him and have him and the kids in danger. It was only logical that she'd send the key to her best friend," I said, and frowned at her. "Some best friend."

"Well, I wouldn't worry about it all too much, Mavis. You can't prove any of this." She pushed her chair out from the table.

"Wait, Madge. I'm not finished. Did you kill Tammy, too?"

She looked at me sharply. "No!" Her voice came out like a hiss.

"She went on the cruise with you, didn't she? If I'd asked her, she would have known you'd have had the opportunity to kill Elizabeth."

"Yes, but she took Elizabeth's place as my best friend. Besides, she didn't know anything about the rest of it."

"You mean the rest of what you were doing? Blackmailing Vernon Spencer? If you didn't kill her, then he must have thought it was Tammy. He probably suspected all along that she knew something more than she was saying. What were you doing, feeding him the evidence a little at a time? Extorting money for each document? You got Tammy killed, you know that, Madge?"

"Shut up, Mavis!" She stood and picked up her purse.

"Where are you hiding what's left, Madge?" I almost shouted at her. "In your house? And how's Robert going to feel about you when I tell him what I know?"

Madge sank back down, her purse in her lap. "You aren't going to tell him anything, Mavis. You're coming with me."

"The hell you say." I'd always wanted to use that line.

"I've got a gun, Mavis," she said in a low voice. "I killed Elizabeth, and it won't bother me much to get rid of you, too. As far as I'm concerned, you're just another obstacle in my way."

"You admit you killed her then?" I asked with a smile.

"Yes, I did. She was coming back, she said. She was waiting on the Texas Rangers to make their move, and then she was coming back. She was going to take Robert away from me, and my babies, too."

"The Texas Rangers?"

Madge made a little movement and so did I. I was hoping she wasn't going to shoot me right then and there. I have to admit to one thing: butterflies—huge swallowtails—flapping their wings madly in my stomach.

"Don't move, Mavis. I'm not too good with guns."

My stomach lurched, but I was cool. "Tell me about the Texas Rangers."

"Who gives a damn," she said. "Let's go."

"It's no skin off your nose, Madge. I'm just curious, that's all."

"Shit! I guess it won't hurt to tell you at this point. They're the ones who helped her get to Houston. They've got a man in the DA's office, she said. Of course she told me all this before she realized why I went to see her." Madge chuckled then, and I got some small inkling as to how far off her rocker she'd fallen.

I wondered who the man in the DA's office was. Hopefully Mike. To Madge I reacted, "Wow! How'd you expect to get away with killing her then?"

She glanced around the almost-empty mall area. That made me a might nervous. I was afraid she'd be suspicious if she saw Ben, but he was sipping his coffee at Uncle Charlie's behind us and ostensibly had his nose buried in a newspaper.

"I figured they'd think Vern found her and did it. He had enough motive."

"God, Madge! Doesn't anything bother you? You'd have let Vernon Spencer take the rap for her murder?"

"He's nothing but a dope dealer and a double-crosser, Mavis. He deserves to be punished!"

"And you don't?" Her logic was astounding.

"I didn't mean to kill her," she said almost convincingly.

"Nah! The panty hose just wrapped itself around her neck by itself."

"Oh, forget it! I thought you'd understand. She was going to take Robert and my girls away from me. I'm their real mother. Not her. I'm the one who took care of them. Not her. I told her I had the files, and that she couldn't come back, but she just laughed at me. Laughed at me! After all those years we'd been friends." Madge was fidgeting with her purse. "She said the Texas Rangers had a copy and that it wouldn't be too much longer before it would all be cleared up."

Madge was getting a kind of crazy, glazed expression in her eyes. My stomach flip-flopped again. It was time to bail out. I nodded my head slightly at Ben, and then kept my eyes on Madge's. I'd always seen in the westerns that if you watch their eyes, you can tell when they're going to draw their gun. I hoped I could tell when she was going to fire hers.

"Come on, Mavis. No more stalling," she said, and her eyes grew as round as silver dollars.

"Don't look now, Madge, but my boyfriend is right behind you."

"Sure." She gave me a disbelieving look. "Let's go, Mavis. Stand up."

I looked at Ben, who had almost reached her, and shrugged my shoulders.

"Don't try anything, Mavis," she said, standing up again. This time her right hand was inside her purse.

"I'm not going to do anything, Madge." I put my hands in the air. "But you better put your purse down. You're covered from several angles and shooting me won't do you any good."

"She's right, ma'am," Ben said in his husky voice as he came up behind her. He grabbed one of her wrists in each hand. The purse fell away, and sure enough, she did have a small pistol in her hand. "Drop it, lady," Ben ordered, and his knuckles turned white as he squeezed his hand tighter on hers and forced the gun downward, much to my immense relief.

She let go of the handgun and struggled, her face contorted with hatred as she glared at me, and Ben cuffed her hands behind her back. Then another man walked up, flashed a badge at Madge, and said "Texas Department of

Public Safety, ma'am." As he took her away, he was reading from a card with the Miranda warning on it, advising her of her rights.

"Sit down and have a doughnut, Ben. We have some time before we have to be at the district attorney's office." I smiled up at him. My hero.

After he got another cup of coffee, Ben sat with me, his huge brown eyes shining as he smiled and shook his head at my obvious glee.

"This is fun, isn't it, Ben?"

"Sure, Mavie," he said, and, reaching over, stroked the bandages on my face. "If you like people wanting to shoot you. And if you like getting all messed up."

"It's not so bad. Is it?" I wished I'd stopped to put on some makeup. I knew there were ugly scratches on the parts of my face not hidden by bandages.

"I guess not. I just keep wondering what you would have done without me. She would have shot you."

"I know. I wouldn't have met her like this if you hadn't turned up. I suppose I would have had to go to the grand jury."

"Suppose you had talked to the wrong DA about it?" He cupped my cheek in his hand. "Suppose they decided to get rid of you?"

"I know. I've been doing a lot of supposing. I guess I could have called you for advice. I did call you, in fact." I grinned at him. Up to then we hadn't discussed our personal lives.

"When?"

"Three times. Twice before you called me and once after. You were never there."

He grinned, his eyes creasing at the corners, the lines around his mouth becoming smile wrinkles. "I'm glad to hear that. Maybe I'm making some progress with you."

"Maybe. Want to make some more?"

"Sure," he grinned.

"Don't give me a hard time the rest of today. I know you don't like what I'm about to do, but don't fight me. I know what I'm doing and, with the men you've lined up, everything will work out." I held his hand and stared into his eyes with my best pleading expression.

"You're hopeless, Mavis."

"I know, but I'm cute. Right?"

"Yeah," he said and sighed exaggeratedly. "Dangerous, but cute."

"Hey, did you hear what Madge said about the Texas Rangers?"

He had just swallowed from his cup and shook his head. "She said Elizabeth was in touch with them and that they have a man in the DA's office."

"If that's the case—"

"No you don't, Ben. We don't know who it is, and we're all set. No stalling."

"But if I call their local office, maybe I could find out."

"Sure, and if they're as slow as they've been for the past year, we'll miss our chance."

"We really should."

"I thought you had no great affection for the Texas Rangers," I said with a smirk.

"I don't."

"Then don't call. They'll just screw things up. Or worse, order us to stay out of it."

I could tell Ben didn't really want to contact them. He just felt a moral obligation. I, on the other hand, didn't have any morals. "Please?" I asked again in my little girl voice.

"O—kay. Let's go get Spencer."

Chapter 31

"IS DOYLE PROCTOR IN?" I ASKED the receptionist behind the window at the entrance to the district attorney's office.

"Yes," said the young lady, the glass enclosure making her voice sound hollow. "I'm sorry. I don't remember your name."

"Mavis Davis." She didn't know it, but her statement made my day. I watched while she picked up the phone, punched a button, and said something.

"You can go on back," she said when she hung up.

I passed through the second glass door and found Proctor's office. "Hi," I said as I entered.

He was standing next to his desk. "Hello, Miss Davis. Have a seat. I've been expecting you." He was dressed in a brown silk suit with a brown and blue paisley silk tie knotted loosely at the neck of his button-down collar shirt. On his feet he wore what looked like $500 cowboy boots, made of some kind of reptile. Poor thing.

"You have?" For a minute I thought he was onto me. I studied his face for a moment. It wouldn't do to let on how nervous he made me. I'd just have to go on with my charade. I smiled nonchalantly. The little voice in my head was telling me to turn and run out the door. I even went so far as reaching for the door before I recovered my composure. "Oh, you mean because of last night. You've been in touch with those nice deputies, I guess. May I close the door?"

"Be my guest."

I shut the door and we both sat down. I took the chair directly opposite him. "Yeah, it was pretty scary last night, both times, but I think I've got this thing figured out, and I need your help," I said as I looked as earnestly as I could into his eyes.

"I'll do everything in my power," he said.

"And that's saying a lot, I know, because as the chief assistant district attorney you're one of the most powerful men in the county." I prayed that he was as susceptible to a snow job as any other man.

"It's kind of you to say so," he said, a pleased expression on his face.

He was. "Not at all," I said with a small smile. "Now, let me tell you what I've figured out about this thing."

"Please do." He sat back, making a tent with his fingers.

"Well, at first, I had a tendency to believe the Houston Police Department's theory of how Elizabeth was murdered or, rather, the why of it, except that I found out from a friend that the other women who were victims of the serial killer had been raped, and she wasn't. That's what convinced me that I should look into the case."

He didn't say anything. He stroked his chin and nodded like Soloman listening to testimony in the temple.

"The most puzzling thing has always been why she would hide out. Why would a married woman with two children, especially a successful lawyer, run away and hide out? Of course it took me a little while to figure out that she was married and all. But then I eventually found my way up here and found out all that stuff. Prior to that, though, I learned that she had a safe deposit box to which one of the keys was missing. I gave it my best shot, but never turned up the second key. Neither did Houston's finest." I grinned as I thought of the exchange I'd had with Lon Tyler. "Are you following me?"

He nodded again, his eyes watching me.

"Anyway, the box was oversized for what it contained, which indicated that it must have been leased for something larger, which must have been removed at one time or another. I put that together with the fact that one of the keys was missing, and I concluded that she had given the key to someone that she trusted—just in case something happened to her."

His poker face remained expressionless. He was totally cool. He didn't even doodle on his desk pad.

"So I had to figure out who would get the key. Not her family, 'cause if she ever came into contact with any of them, they were likely to try to persuade her to come home, and there was a sound reason why she couldn't. Whatever she was hiding was her protection. I believe that she was working on finding someone honest that she could trust. Are you following me? I know I'm rambling, but you need to know all this."

He nodded again. "I've got you so far. Go ahead."

I leaned back in my chair and pulled out a cigarette. It was a long story. I might as well enjoy the telling of it. I lit my cigarette, smiled at Proctor, and continued. I don't need to mention how excited I was.

"So anyway, I figured whoever she had trusted had turned on her for one reason or another and I had to figure out who that person was. Right off, I was suspicious of Vernon Spencer. The first day I was here I met some people who had known Elizabeth for years, and they didn't like him. Of course I wasn't sure if their dislike was connected to a particular incident or his race or whether they truly had a valid reason that involved Elizabeth.

"A bit later, a former client of Elizabeth's told me he suspected her of stealing his dope. Shocked me, I can tell you. Remember I told you about him? Anyway, I checked that out, and there was no way. I mean, she just wasn't the type, what with her history of fighting against it and all, so I figured that she suspected that Spencer was into dope. For a long time she must have documented what Spencer was doing. I believe he was taking dope instead of fees and selling it. Probably charging more than he would have if the fee had been cash since he still had the risk of selling it." There were a few ideas that I had that I didn't reveal. I was hoping for confirmation of that later on. "I think that Elizabeth must have confronted him and he must have threatened her, either go in with him or else, so she ran."

Proctor sat up in his chair and leaned at me. "Can you prove that? If so, we've got him. I've suspected something like that for a long time. He just seems to be doing too well financially."

I put my hand up to halt his enthusiasm. "Hold that thought. I'm getting to that. The deal was that she had this client that thought she was the one who he'd heard made dope deals to get people out of jail, but it was Spencer instead. It was an easy mistake. I figure from what the client, Thompson, said, that he left a message at her office and Spencer got it instead of her. Tammy may have known that. Anyway, when Elizabeth realized it, that was when she confronted Spencer and that's how it all began. But, as I found out later, Spencer was in trial against you at the time of the murder. He could have killed her except for that. Catherine, her daughter, had told her dad that she was writing to her mom care of general delivery in Dickinson, which is south of Houston. Robert thought Spencer could do no wrong and spilled the beans to both Spencer and Madge. It would have been easy for anyone to have gone down there, if they had the time, and wait for her to show up, and follow her. It would have been boring and tedious, but easy."

"But you say Spencer wasn't able to because he was in trial with me?"

"Yeah, his secretary told me that he'd been in trial for weeks. I checked the monthly docket sheet, and it's true. In fact, you two were still at it when I got here, remember? Elizabeth was killed the first part of the week before I arrived. Spencer couldn't have been down there waiting for her."

"That's right."

I put my cigarette out and smiled at him. "But don't worry, the best friend did it. Madge Hennesey. That's what I'm getting to."

His face showed mild surprise, but then he reached for the phone. "Let me get an investigator in here, and I'll have her picked up."

"No, no, you mustn't do that," I said as I jumped up and put my hand on his. "If you do that, we may never flush Spencer out over the drug thing. And what about Tammy Bradley? I don't figure that Madge killed her. And then, too, there were at least two people shooting at Mr. Thompson and me last night."

He released the phone and let it fall back into its cradle. "You have a plan?" His smooth complexion actually wrinkled a bit as he waited to hear me out.

"Yeah. See, I figure that Spencer thinks that Willard Thompson now knows that he took his dope. The way I figure it, Spencer stole Thompson's dope and then the court appointed Spencer to represent Thompson." I sat back down across from him and took a deep breath. "It said so on Thompson's docket sheet. It was awkward, at best, but Spencer made him plead out for pen time. Then, when Thompson found out that it wasn't there anymore— the dope, I mean—and when he recently found out from me that Elizabeth probably hadn't taken it, he figured out that it was Spencer who took it." I pounded on his desk. "That's why Spencer tried to shoot him last night, and me, too, coupled with the fact that he has to know that we now know that he's into dope dealing. Spencer probably thinks Thompson told me. So what we have to do is try to trick Spencer, and then we can catch him and Madge at the same time. Understand?"

"I think so, but how will you do that?" He looked at me with one eyebrow cocked. It seemed he was human after all. Did I have him worried?

"I think Madge has been blackmailing him with the stuff she got out of Elizabeth's safe deposit box. He probably thought it was Tammy, and that's why he killed her, but it was Madge."

"Jesus Christ! I never would have suspected Vernon Spencer of murder."

"Yeah, right. So, here's the deal. I figure that Madge has the evidence hidden somewhere in her house. Spencer still thinks it was Tammy. He's probably worried now about where Tammy put it. I'll call him and tell him to meet me. I'll disguise my voice. I'm sure that's what she did, because one night I got a call like that. Anyway, then I'll call Madge and ask her to meet me, but I won't be there. I'll be at Madge's and I'll get in and get the evidence I need against Spencer. It'll also be what we need to convict Madge of murder. Spencer will show up to meet whoever the blackmailer is, and

Madge will be there, because that's where I'll send her. If I find the evidence, we'll have enough to arrest and convict both of them."

"That sounds awfully complicated. Why don't I just get a search warrant and go out to her place and see if it's there?" he asked, his voice and face passive again.

"Because if it's not, she'll be on to you, and be able to destroy it, and then we'll never get her or him."

"That's true, but if I authorize you to do this, that's burglary of a habitation."

"So don't authorize me, Mr. Proctor. Just don't stop me. I'm a private citizen. If I find the evidence, it can be used in court. I'm not asking your permission and you aren't directing me. I'm just letting you in on what I'm going to do. Your people can't go in without authorization and expect to use it against them, so it has to be me. If I get caught, you don't want the blame, do you?" I maintained as serious a look as possible.

"No, and I'll deny any knowledge of it."

"Exactly." I was sure he would.

"Okay. Have you got your timing down? When do you expect to pull this off?"

"I'd say around dinner time. Just after dark. I only hope she hasn't hidden the evidence elsewhere."

"Right. And then if you find it, you're going to give me a call so I can have some men pick them up?"

"Yes. As soon as I get it and get clear of the house, okay? You'll be here when I call?"

"Right here waiting," he said. "I won't leave until I hear from you." He stood up and held out his hand for me to shake. "Miss Davis, you're a genius."

I took his hand. I didn't want to, but I did. "So nice of you to say so." If I was right about what I really thought, he probably wouldn't be saying such complimentary things about me later.

We parted company. When I got downstairs, Ben picked me up. He'd been busy lining up a few more guys. I have to admit that having Ben around does come in handy sometimes.

We found Madge's address. It was a little house just outside of Richland Hills, an exclusive subdivision for the wealthy. It wasn't difficult to position *our* men around the neighborhood, on the streets, and in driveways. Everybody came in unmarked cars.

Ben and I sat in the front seat of his Ford in the driveway of a house across and down the street from Madge's. We sipped soft drinks while we waited.

"I still hope you're wrong, Mavis," he said. His mouth formed a grim line. His eyes darted up and down the street.

"So do I, Ben, but everything points to it. Proctor may not be as deeply involved as Spencer, but he's got to be the one. I just hope Miguel Mirales, the investigator, isn't in on it, too. I kind of liked him."

"Oh, yeah?" He rolled his eyes as he said it, feigning jealousy.

"Not like that, Ben." I gave him a playful poke in the arm. "I liked his handshake, and he treated me nicely—like he believed me and that what I was saying had some value."

"You and your handshake theory."

"Well, I'll admit it's not a foolproof method, but most of the time I can tell about people like that. I did like Madge, though, too. She was quite a character." I shrugged and stared out the window.

"Sometimes this isn't fun, is it?"

"Nope." I lit a cigarette, but Ben didn't say anything this time. I rolled down the window, and we waited. It was approaching noon. The air was still and hot. An old man in the next block was cutting his grass, his power mower making us speak loudly.

"I still hope it's not him," Ben said again later. "A prosecutor." He shook his head.

"Don't you see? It has to be. Why else would Elizabeth have been so scared? If she knew it was someone else, she could have gone to Proctor—reported Spencer, but with Proctor being chief assistant, she didn't know how much it had spread or who she could trust."

As if to confirm what I'd just said, a familiar dark sedan turned down the road. Ben radioed to the other guys, and we slid down in our seats. The car slowed as it approached Madge's house, then turned into the driveway and stopped.

Vernon Spencer got out on the passenger side.

"That's Vernon Spencer," I whispered to the back of Ben's head.

Doyle Proctor got out on the driver's side.

"Doyle Proctor," I whispered.

The back door to the sedan opened, but it wasn't Miguel Mirales who got out. It was Ray something-or-other, Mike's office mate. Ben turned his head toward me and caught me grinning.

"That's not Mike Mirales."

Ben smiled and whispered, "You're just lucky sometimes."

We waited and watched as they fooled with the front-door lock for a minute before going inside the house. A while later they emerged. Proctor was carrying a long, thick, manila envelope. They were grinning. Spencer laughed at something Proctor was saying.

They returned to their car, backed into the street, and started off down the road. A white sedan pulled out of a driveway in front of them, blocking their exit. A blue sedan pulled up from around the corner behind them. Two men got out of each car and stood behind the doors, guns drawn. Somebody hollered.

We were too far away to hear exactly what was being said, but we knew the general content. The doors of the black sedan opened and the three men got out with their hands up. It was over.

Later that afternoon, I found out that Mike was the Texas Ranger inside. I was glad. He tried to be angry that we didn't include his agency, but he got over it. After all, the Texas Rangers are sort of the elite of the Texas Department of Public Safety, so they sort of were included.

We also found out that Spencer was into three separate things: taking dope in exchange for legal services, selling dope, and, if he heard of a particularly nice cache, setting up the other dealers for a bust. Ray and Spencer were in on that together: Ray would be in on the bust, with a few other cops, and they'd skim some drugs off the top before they filed the official inventory. For example, if it was coke worth a mil on the street, by the time they got through with their inventory, it was worth half. Good deal if you can get it, I guess.

Mike had been real close to completing the operation when Elizabeth was killed. Her death complicated things.

Tammy Bradley was just an error all the way around.

Unhappily, that's the way it goes sometimes.

Later that afternoon, I checked in with my office.

"Good afternoon. Mavis Davis Productions is our name, creative solutions is our game. What may we do for your edification today?" came the high-pitched voice over the wire.

I cringed. What had I done? Created a monster? I wanted to hang up, crawl away, and change my name. How could Margaret do this to me? I started counting backwards from ten. I knew the girl was sensitive, and I was about to lose all control.

"Hello? Is anybody there?" she sang out.

Three, two, one. "If you ever answer the phone like that again, Margaret Applebaum, I will kill you," I said into the phone. "And there won't be any mystery about who did it either."

"Gee, I'm sorry, Mavis," she whined. "Candy and I thought it would add character to the place."

"Believe me when I tell you that the office has enough character already."

"Okay. I was just trying to help," her voice had taken on a nasal quality.

Tears, I didn't need. "Margaret, listen to me carefully. I've finished with the Elizabeth Reynolds case and will be coming home tomorrow after I talk to a few people, make some phone calls, and tie up some loose ends." And get my tires replaced, I wanted to say. But I wasn't going into that right now.

"Elizabeth Reynolds. Who's that?"

Saints preserve us. "Doris Jones, Margaret."

"Oh! You found out who killed her, Mavis? Gee, that's really great!"

"Yeah. Right. Will you call Carl and tell him, and tell him that I'll get together with him after I get home and explain it to him?"

"How can I explain it to him, Mavis, when I don't know what happened?"

I shook my head before I continued struggling with the conversation. It was a good thing that I was over two hundred miles away.

Thank you for reading!

If you enjoyed *My First Murder*, I would appreciate it if you would help others to enjoy this book, too.

Share it with a friend.

Recommend it. Please help others find this book by recommending it to friends, readers' groups, and discussion boards.

Review it. Please tell other readers why you liked this book by reviewing it at Amazon or Goodreads. If you do write a review, please send me an email at susan@susanpbaker.com so I can thank you with a personal email.

If you would like to be on my mailing list so you can receive news of upcoming events and publications, go to www.susanpbaker.com

ABOUT THE AUTHOR

Susan P. Baker, a retired Texas judge, is the author of six novels and two nonfiction books, all related to the law. As a judge, she dealt with murder, kidnapping, incest, stalking, child support, child custody, and divorce. Prior thereto, she practiced law for nine years and, while in law school, worked as a probation officer. Her experience in the justice system is apparent in her writings. Currently, she has two mysteries and two suspense novels in progress.

Susan is a member of Texas Authors, Authors Guild, Sisters in Crime, Writers League of Texas, and Galveston Novel and Short Story Writers.

She has two children and eight grandchildren. She loves dark chocolate, raspberries, and traveling. An anglophile, she likes to visit cousins in England and Australia (her mother was a British war bride). On her bucket list are a trip to New Zealand, a long trip back to Australia, living in England for several months at a time, visiting all the presidential libraries and authors' homes in the U.S., and driving Route 66.

Read more about Susan and sign up for her mailing list at
http://www.susanpbaker.com
Like her at http://www.facebook.com/legalwriter
Follow her on Twitter @Susanpbaker.

Made in the USA
Columbia, SC
23 May 2019